What Haunts the Heart

What Haunts the Heart

Obsession, Regrets and Fractured Souls

Edited by Matthew Pegg

First published in the UK in 2016 by Mantle Lane Press

ISBN e-book edition 978-0-9932648-2-5
ISBN print edition   978-0-9932648-1-8

Mantle Lane Press
Mantle Arts
Springboard Centre
Mantle Lane
Coalville
LE67 3DW
www.mantlelanepress.co.uk
www.red-lighthouse.org.uk

Cover image by The Dunce
www.thedunce.co.uk

Contents

Introduction

We all create our own ghosts. We make them from the stuff of the past, from relationships that crashed and burned or never began, from our mistakes and our choices, the roads we never took or the ones we took too readily, from our broken promises and the things we lost along the way. We give life to our ghosts and allow them to haunt us. For some, they become all consuming. Mostly they are in our heads. Perhaps some are not...

The writers in this collection bring unique perspectives to the theme of being haunted. Here you will find stories of lost loves, regrets, poor decisions, madness, secrets, obsession, and redemption.

What Haunts the Heart collects together historical and literary fiction, contemporary fantasy, psychological horror, and, of course, ghost stories.

Matthew Pegg
February 2016

Tiger Moth
Graham Joyce

Lenny suspected that other lawyers were passing him mad clients. He was known around town for his soft-shell, and neither the competition nor his own firm were above abusing his good nature. Not that he hadn't passed over a funny-farm client or a litigious bore himself. That was in the mix, everybody did it if the file got too long or if they were getting through too many cans of air-freshener after taking an affidavit. But fair is fair and bad law had to be spread around evenly.

Lenny was a matrimonial solicitor in the Norfolk seaside town of Hunstanton. He occupied an office cluttered with files, framed photographs and obsolete law books belonging to a senior partner who himself occupied a minimalist, dust-free suite across the hall. Plucking up his gold-nibbed ink fountain pen, a theatrical prop he kept to impress the likes of his present client, Lenny put the question. "Mrs Grapes, why you do think the man you are living with is not your husband?"

"I already told you. He was very thin when we got married. Slim as a cigarette. I don't know what happened to my real husband. I don't know where this man came from." Mrs Grapes dabbed her eyes with the tissue Lenny had given her.

"And when did this fatness occur?"

Mrs Grapes blinked at the question. In truth, Lenny did too. He couldn't remember when in the last dozen years of legal practice he had phrased such a bad question. The fact is he wasn't paying proper attention. He was trying to remember which of his legal 'friends' had steered him the case.

Mrs Grapes, herself thin to the point of a disturbingly translucent skin, shifted on her bony haunches and tried to frame a reply.

"Mrs Grapes," Lenny said, making it easier for her, "are you absolutely certain that this man is not your husband?"

"I told you already. I married a thin man, not this huge fat person. I want a divorce."

Lenny looked at the door, the window, the small ventilator panel in the upper corner of the room: all the usual means of egress. As Mrs Grapes outlined her suspicions further, he fought a noisy internal dialogue about how he might tactfully get her out of the room, legally and with kindness.

Whenever Lenny found himself in a legal grey area, a point at which the meaning of the law might have to be massaged to fit, he had a give-away habit of shaping his mouth into an O before speaking. "Mrs Grapes, if this man is masquerading as your husband then it's a criminal matter not a civil one."

"Oh?"

"That's correct, Mrs Grapes. I have to advise you on a point of law that you can't divorce this man because you never married him."

"Oh?"

Lenny got out of his seat and came round the table. "Indeed. You can't go around divorcing people you never married in the first place. And you do after all seem certain he's not the man you married. Mrs Grapes, what you need is the police. Who will be vigorous in their efforts to help you."

He was already gently raising Mrs Grapes by her elbow out of her chair and leading her to the anteroom to his office. There the secretary Lenny shared with the firm's senior partner tried to slip a gardening magazine onto her knees. She was known as 'the redoubtable Susan', an epithet that baffled Lenny. "Susan, could you look after my client? Mrs Grapes, my secretary here will give you the number of the police station."

"I will," Susan said, "but I'm very stressed."

Mrs Grapes, impressed that her case warranted immediate police attention rather than the lumbering machinery of the law, seemed grateful and happy to leave. Lenny closed his office door, sank back in his seat and pulled off his tie.

Moments later Susan walked in without knocking and dumped a pile of new files on his desk. "What's this?" he asked.

"Mr Falconer is hard pressed and wanted you to take these extra cases on. You're lucky I brought them. I shouldn't be carrying all of these things, what with my back."

"No, Susan."

After she had left, Lenny made a call.

"Simon, is that job in Nottingham still available?"

Simon had studied law with Lenny at Nottingham Trent University. Lenny was best man at his wedding. Simon's wife Elizabeth was always trying to fix Lenny up romantically. Beautiful, kind Elizabeth, on whom Lenny secretly doted, didn't think a thirty-five year old man should still be living with his mother and told him so, often. "I spoke to George only yesterday. Said he's very keen to see you."

"Know what? I've been in this town too long."

"They dump on you Lenny. What happened now?"

"Nothing. Just don't let Elizabeth see your fat-rolls."

After talking to Simon, Lenny put a call through to the Nottingham legal firm of Chortleman & Brace, to arrange an informal lunch date for the following day. Then he asked the redoubtable Susan to re-arrange all his morning appointments.

Susan made an unnecessary venting noise. "I will but I'm very stressed." Susan shopped at the same stores as Lenny's mother. She wore long kilts and lacy blouses, and kept a tiny tissue tucked inside her sleeve. Susan hauled herself out of her typing chair and made her kilt swing aggressively as she stepped over to the filing cabinet. The cabinet drawer was rattled opened and banged shut. The relevant files thwacked her desk. "Very stressed."

"Yes," said Lenny. "I can see that."

Mrs Grapes was Lenny's last client of the day. He gathered up the burden of the new files to take home and slipped out of the back door, trying to be discreet as he shuffled across the car park to his Saab. He sat behind the wheel for a moment wondering how he might break the news to his mother that he was considering a job in Nottingham.

"Well, you know best," his mother said.

She'd just served up a familiar dinner of steamed haddock, mashed potatoes and peas. Lenny looked through the steam rising from the fish, saw his mother compress her lips, and regretted blurting out his news. His stomach squeezed. He knew he wouldn't be able to eat one forkful of the meal before him. The worst of all possible responses was to hear his Mother say that he, Lenny, knew best. When Lenny knew best, his mother often set her features and said not a single word for several days.

"It's just a preliminary discussion. An exploration. They probably won't even offer me the job."

His mother said nothing to that, hacking at her fish as if it were tough steak.

Lenny and his mother had relocated to the coastal town of Hunstanton shortly after his father had died of an unexpected aneurysm when Lenny was nine years old. His mother couldn't face the old house. It reminded her too much of the husband she'd lost. In fact she hadn't coped too well with the new life either, and Lenny soon became the man of the house, with an emotionally dependent mother. Lenny had missed the opportunity to escape through studying for a law degree. He made the fatal mistake of moving back in with his mother when he was offered a job in his home town. Several years on Mrs Pearce still baked and iced cup cakes and sprinkled them with hundreds-and-thousands every Sunday afternoon. Lenny's favourites, she said. She made his cocoa every night at nine-thirty in the evening. Lenny's routine. She washed and pressed all of his clothes for him, and she even pressed his socks. Lenny's preference.

When Lenny had first mentioned the idea of Nottingham, his mother had laid down the fish slice and said, "But think of the commuting time! You'd have to drive right around The Wash and then across the country. All of those winding roads!"

"Well I'd stay in Nottingham,' Lenny had said. Then, too late and unable to save himself, as he saw her stiffen he'd added, "Except for week-ends."

Lenny pushed his food around on his plate before retiring to his room. Not fond of the lace frills and cotton flounces and ubiquitous glass ornaments favoured by his mother, he often beat a retreat to the sanctuary of his bedroom. There he lay on his bed, hands folded behind his head, staring up at the model aeroplanes suspended from the ceiling by invisible lengths of cotton.

But Lenny knew best. And while even the sweetest but some-what possessive mother might say, "Right then, wash and press your own stinky socks buster, and your shirt and trousers too", Lenny's mother rose in the morning, still marbled in silence, and laid out his shirt and tie, polished his shoes til they gleamed and brushed down his best dark suit.

"It's not an interview Mum, it's a chat. My jacket will be more comfortable."

"You know best, Leonard." She hung the suit back in his wardrobe, took down the jacket and began to brush it for lint with stiff, downward strokes. Then she held it for him to slip into.

"I'll be back mid-afternoon, Mum."

"As you wish."

Mrs Pearce opened the door for her son but failed to offer her cheek for the ritual peck. He kissed her anyway and hurried to his Saab. Lenny glanced back before he drove away. His mother, motionless, watched from the window.

His mother was entirely correct about the drive to Nottingham. It was necessary to hug the coastal rode to King's Lynn, through the flat reclaimed land around The Wash before cutting across fen land on the way over to Nottingham. It was a winding drive alongside grassy dikes and irrigation ditches, past muddy reed-beds and canals teeming with eels under the open sky of Lincolnshire; a wind-blasted land reeking of brine. It was a land much beloved by Lenny, but which had one day mysteriously become his prison.

At a service station he stopped to fill up the tank, loitering, already early for his appointment. In the washroom he looked hard at his gentle, slightly pudgy features, wondering if he could slim himself down to a completely different person, one who might replace a woman's husband or a mother's son. His hand strayed to the red-and-yellow metal badge pinned to his lapel. He considered removing it, wondering if it made him look childish. But he left it. The badge was, after all, talismanic. It was a badge of a De Havilland Tiger Moth biplane. He'd found it in the grass shortly after he'd moved to the area with his mother almost twenty-five years earlier, on what had been a momentous day.

It was shortly after his father had died and the first time he and his mother had ventured out of their new home together. He'd had to beg her to take him out of a house rattling with his father's ghost, even though his father had never lived there. His mother had trailed the ghost all the way to Hunstanton. She never let a day go by without referring to his father or without making him the standard by which Lenny should measure his life.

Then Lenny hit upon the expedient of saying, "Dad would have liked it." He was learning to fight ghosts with ghosts. So his mother, dragging chains she'd made for herself, had made a brief, nervous drive to the beach. There she sat in a deck chair, knees pressed together, sweltering in a woollen cardigan. She'd made Lenny swear he wouldn't stray too far from the beach, already exhibiting a terror of being left alone out of doors, even for an hour.

But Lenny had of course strayed behind the beach and over the dunes to the coastal road. On the other side of the road was a steep grassy dike, and on the dike two boys were beating tremendous fun out of a giant cardboard box. The boys carried the box to the crest of the dike, climbed inside it and then powered themselves down the slope. In a pitch of raucous laughter they were spilled into the dry gully at the foot of the dike before dragging the box back up the gradient and repeating the ride. The boys, both about his own age, made it seem the most uproarious fun a boy could have in the world, and in watching them Lenny felt the deep sting of loneliness.

He ventured across the road.

With another ride imminent one of the boys shouted from the top of the hill. "There's another Willard, Willard."

"Aye Willard," said the smaller of the boys. "Looks to me like a Willard, Willard."

"Come aboard Willard!" shouted the first boy. He beckoned Lenny on.

Lenny looked behind him for someone who might be called Willard. The dunes were utterly deserted, and the road was clear. The sun baked down, and seemed to move a notch in the sky, as if operated on a ratchet. Lenny squinted back at the boys, whose white shirts flared in the brilliant sunlight.

"Yes, you Willard!" said the first boy. "Come aboard! We're about to let her rip!"

"Look sharp Willard," said his companion. "You don't want to miss this!"

Lenny glanced behind him again, stupidly. There was no one there. The two boys were indeed talking to him, gazing down at him, expectant, as if his decision to join them were momentous. Lenny began climbing the steep grassy bank.

"Hurrah, Willard's joining us!"

"Good chap Willard, climb aboard, plenty of room!"

Lenny panted at the top of the slope. "My name isn't Willard."

The first boy, older with sleek black hair and liquid dark eyes shouted, "He says his name isn't Willard, Willard."

"Of course it's Willard, Willard." His pal had a wild tousle of brown hair and a face full of freckles. "Jump in Willard. There's a chap."

Lenny got in anyway. It was a squeeze, but he saw that he could slide his legs around the boy in front.

"Willard's maiden flight!" yelled the dark-haired boy. "Fuel levels?"

"Check," his friend returned.

"Altimeter?"

"Check"

"Confubulator?"

"Check."

"Choks away!"

They pushed off. The box slipped easily down the slope, propelled by the weight of the three boys. It gathered speed as it went, then as it hit the gully at the bottom it pitched the three boys right out of the box into a clattering, giggling heap.

"All okay Willard 2?" shouted the slightly older boy.

"Okay," replied the freckled lad.

"Okay Willard 3?" He stared hard at Lenny.

"Okay."

"Good! Then once more to the breach!"

Everything about the boys' behaviour and speech was puzzling, but was compensated for by the scale of hysterical fun afforded by the brief ride in the cardboard box. Even if their phrases belonged to a forgotten time, the warmth and friendly overtures exhibited by the boys was startling in contrast to the usual surliness and hostility common to most boys of that age.

"The new Willard is a good egg, Willard."

"Jolly good egg Willard."

"My name's not Willard, it's Lenny."

The older boy stopped in his tracks. He set down the box, put an arm round Lenny's shoulder and spoke confidentially. "Look, it's a crashing bore isn't it, when you come on holiday, to learn another chap's name. Far easier if everyone is called Willard. I'm Willard 1, my brother is Willard 2, you're Willard 3. Right Willard?"

Lenny met the boy's swimming dark eyes full on. "Understood Willard."

"The new Willard catches on fast, Willard."

"Three cheers for the new Willard!"

And after cheers, the cardboard box runs went on and on and, if the baking sun slipped a further notch in the sky, none of the boys noticed. The box runs went on until disaster struck, when Willard 1 noticed the loss of a pin-badge.

"It must have come off in the grass."

"What's it look like?" Lenny asked.

"It's a biplane. We're going to be fighter pilots when we're grown up. Isn't that right Willard?"

"Right Willard."

Lenny wasn't sure what a biplane was but didn't like to ask. As for fighter pilots, his only notion of a career was that his mother had told him he was going to be a doctor or a lawyer. In any event, together the three of them combed the grass without success. And in that time the shadow of the dike crept longer.

Willard 1 seemed especially depressed at losing his pin-badge, but hunting for it was a lost cause. The search was interrupted when there came the sound of an engine in the sky, approaching from seaward. The three boys looked up. It was an old-fashioned biplane flying low, chugging over their heads, it's engine popping, low enough to see the pilot in his leathers.

"It's a De Havilland!" shouted Willard 1, as if astonished. "What a stroke of luck!"

"A Tiger Moth!" shrieked Willard 2, barely able to contain his excitement.

Lenny, to whom these words meant nothing, shielded his eyes from the sun and looked up at the double-winged craft soaring overhead.

"But that must be a sign!" shouted Willard 2 to his brother. "Don't you see? You just lost a Tiger Moth pin-badge, and then one flies right overhead! It's a sign!"

"By God you're right Willard!" He turned and watched the biplane chug away from them, trailing clouds of vapour. "We have to follow it!"

The boys ran up over the dike and set off in pursuit of the biplane. "Come on Willard 3!" one of them called without looking back.

Lenny followed an instinct to scramble up the dike after the boys. He saw them chasing across the flat, reedy land as the plane banked and flew off in the direction of the sun. But Lenny faltered, remembering his mother sitting on the beach. He hesitated on the crest of the dike as the biplane disappeared across the horizon. Lenny heard the boys calling as they ran, saw them scramble up a second dike until they too disappeared behind it.

Lenny waited in an ecstasy of indecision. Too late he decided to go after the boys, but when he reached the crest of the second dike he'd lost sight of them. They were nowhere in the vista before him.

He trudged back to the place where the cardboard box lay abandoned. The sun had become like a burnished coin in the sky and the shadows were long. Lenny tried taking a solo ride down the dike, but now the cardboard box was somehow discharged of all its joy. He felt as though he had missed an opportunity among the lords of life; that he'd allowed his mother to chain him back; that he should have gone when they called, wherever they went and whatever the consequences. Moreover, the boys had taken with them the wings of the afternoon and Lenny was left to stand in the cool, creeping shadow of the dike.

But as he put down the box, Lenny found in the grass the lost pin-badge. He kept it as a souvenir, in the hope he might one day encounter the boys again. This souvenir of the afternoon almost compensated for the reception with which his mother greeted him when he returned to the beach.

She turned on him a white-cold fury. "Where have you been?"

"Playing."

"Playing? And didn't it occur to you that I would be sickened and worried senseless while you were playing? And what with your father only dead a few weeks? Didn't it occur to you that I might think you yourself were dead? Didn't it? Didn't it occur to you that I was left here alone? Haven't you anything but selfishness in your heart Leonard? And your father dead just a few weeks and me alone on the beach! Your father would be ashamed of you. Ashamed. He would never, ever, ever leave me alone like that. Never."

"I'm sorry."

But she'd said her piece. And with that she turned on him a silence that had persisted for several days, and it was a punishment that had lasted Lenny a lifetime. It was a pattern repeated when he'd tried to bring girlfriends into his life, or when he'd tried to take a holiday without her. The ghost of his dead father, ashamed at his nine-year-old son's selfishness, never had to be

19

invoked again.

The informal interview went well for Lenny. Chortleman of Chortleman & Brace had retired and George Brace was shaking loose a few cobwebs. He made it easy for Lenny.

"What fees are you earning over there Lenny?"

Lenny told him. Brace blinked. "Substantial caseload?"

Lenny described a caseload that some might call backbreaking. Brace blinked again.

"And what are they paying you?"

Lenny told him. Brace blinked a third time and said, "Hell, Lenny, we'll knock that into a cocked hat."

"Serious?"

"I'm sorry to say this but they're laughing at you. We can up that figure by twenty five per cent, plus we've got health and pension plans we stitched in ourselves. I'll be straight: we need you to run matrimonial. Divorce is booming and yet marriage is still fashionable. Everyone's a winner. Plus summer holidays will be over soon and the caseloads rocket after all that togetherness, you know that. We want you Lenny. Say yes."

"Gosh. I really don't know. I'd have to uproot. It's a lot of fuss."

"Generous re-location package. Full secretarial support. Everything, Lenny."

Lenny promised he'd give it serious thought, and George Brace drove him out to The Millwheel for lunch, where they parked amid the Jags and the Mercs. Over roast duckling and asparagus tips Lenny told George about Mrs Grapes, whose thin husband had been usurped by a fat husband, and George laughed all over the place.

"That's a funny story," George said.

"Sad, too."

"Yes," George agreed. "Sad too."

Lenny took his time over the drive home. He told himself he wanted to suck in the country air but really he was avoiding having to face his mother. He wanted this job like a bird wants the air but he knew he wouldn't take it. It wasn't the first informal interview he'd been to over the years. He just wouldn't be able to look his mother in the eye and tell her that he was leaving her.

As he drove through the waterlands around the fens the sun began to dip, dispatching shadows from the canals and the dikes. He opened his car window to inhale some of the odour of the baked earth and the muddy silt commingled and he decided it was a good smell. Then as he took the coastal road towards Hunstanton he looked across at a steep dike and what he saw made him stop the car and get out.

Two lads cavorted with a cardboard box on the crest of the dike, with the sun dipping behind them. Silhouetted, they played in the exact spot where he'd encountered those other boys almost a quarter-century earlier. Lenny couldn't repress a laugh of recognition.

He made his way over as they came shooting down the dike in the cardboard box, spilling into the gully in gales of laughter. But when he drew up close, the smile disappeared from his lips. One of the lads had sleek black hair and liquid brown eyes. The other had a tousled brown mop and a face full of freckles. They were sprawled now in the shadow of the dike, suddenly aware of him.

"Boys," Lenny said. "Boys." He was standing in strong sunlight, beyond the reach of the dike shadow. He had to shield his eyes from the low sun.

"What?" one of them asked. "What is it?"

But Lenny couldn't speak. It was too absurd. What could he say? He continued to peer at them from beneath the flat visor of his hand. The boys stepped out of the shadow and into the light. Yet even though he was now but a few steps from them, and though they stood in the full glare of the sun, the boys' features remained disguised in half-silhouette. They were the colour of grey slate. A wave of revulsion passed through him.

Then the expression on the boys' faces changed. They looked at him in an ugly manner, suspicious, as if they thought he meant to harm them in some way.

"Look Willard," said the younger of the two. "He's got your pin-badge."

The older boy got to his feet, his face still dark, squinting at the badge on Lenny's lapel. "You're right Willard, how come he's got my badge?"

"Willard!" Lenny shouted, fumbling with the pin-badge, trying to remove it so as to hand it back. "That's it! I remember! Willard!"

"He must be a thief, Willard," said the younger boy. "He must have stolen it!"

"No no no!" Lenny protested. "I found it! Right here in the grass! I never stole it!"

The older boy eyed the badge proffered by Lenny. Then he turned and began scrambling up the dike. "Let's get out of here Willard!"

The second boy followed up the dike. "That's right Willard. We don't want to hang around amongst thieves."

Lenny raced after them. "Wait! I didn't steal it! I want to return it. I've had it all this time!" But his shoes slipped on the grassy bank and his knee collided with the turf and twisted. As he got to his feet, Lenny looked back at the road. A car had slowed down to see what he was doing. He knew he must look ridiculous, a grown man scrambling after two boys.

But he went anyway, and when he got to the top of the gradient he could see the boys already disappearing over the second dike. He followed, and just as before, by the time he'd climbed the second dike, the boys were nowhere to be seen in the flat, marshy expanse before him. The sun dipped behind trees and the landscape was plunged into shadow, and the temperature dropped palpably. And though Lenny's heart was bursting to follow the boys, some other instinct, some life-preserving reflex told him that he mustn't. But as he gazed across the shadowy marshland, with the yellow sun winking behind the charcoal sketch of trees in the distant wood, he heard a piercing bird-like cry of sorrow.

Back in his car, Lenny sat behind the wheel for some time. An hour passed before, with trembling fingers, he re-fixed the pin-badge to his lapel, started the ignition and drove home.

"You're later than I expected," his mother said.

"Yes, it went on."

"I thought something had happened to you on the road. I was worried."

"No. I'm fine and dandy."

She served up dinner. It was cottage pie, carrots and peas, steam billowing upward as she removed it from the hot oven. "I managed to keep this warm. And I've made some gravy."

He peered through the thin cloud coming off the dish, wondering how many dinners of steamed fish and cottage pie he would be made to consume. "Lovely Mother. It looks lovely."

He ate without pleasure, and after he was done he put his knife and fork together neatly on his plate and said in a quiet, firm voice. "I got offered a job in Nottingham. A very good job. I've decided to take it."

She stood up without a word and made to take his plate away, but Lenny said, "No Mum, you sit down, while I tell you about this. You sit down."

She sat and compressed her lips while he looked her in the eye and told her all about the benefits of the job, about Chortleman & Brace, about his plans and about how often he planned to visit her after he'd made the move.

"You know best," was all she would say.

"Yes," Lenny said. "I do. I really do."

Later he went and laid down on his bed, with his hands behind his head, gazing up at the model aeroplanes suspended from the ceiling. He knew that the boys had given him a second chance to follow them. Not into the shade, nor into the mudflats stolen from the sea, not into a land of silhouette, no, none of those dark valleys. But somewhere for himself where he might make his own way.

He thought of his future in Nottingham. He thought of the pin-badge; and of the Tiger Moth biplane; and of where the cavorting boys play forever on the crest of the grassy dike and in its creeping shadow.

Milk Teeth
Emma J. Lannie

It's the same song that was playing the last time I saw my mother. Bassoon, clarinet; that I know the sound of these two instruments is not down to my schooling. There were no private lessons. My mother would dance us around the room, my sister and I, her feet padding softly across the worn rug, and at each new instrument, closed-eyed she would whisper its name: bassoon, clarinet, trumpet. These were the building blocks of the songs that filled our days.

Alexis stands in front of the radio. He has his back to me. His shoulders are rounded. I watch as he begins to shake in that jerky, rhythmic way that tells me his body is crying. He never makes a sound, never lets me see his face when he's like this.

That day, he crushed my ribs with the force of holding me back. The bruises lasted a long time. I was glad of them. They were the only clue that things were wrong. He held me so hard I couldn't breathe. And when he loosened his grip, I fell to my knees and he fell with me. We made a jagged 'S' shape in the dusty street, both of us looking up to where the window, my mother's window, should have been. And it had vanished. The bricks hung there like loose teeth. My mother gone. My sister gone. My sister's name is Clara. She will always be my sister.

I wait for the song to finish. When it does, Alexis stands up straight again, composes himself before turning to me and smiling, like he hasn't been someplace else these past four minutes. I push my thumbs into one of the figs on the table and pick away at the flesh, which I let drop onto the dark, polished oak. My mother's hair was this colour when we lived in England. After six years of living here, though, her hair had grown golden, bleached by the sun, despite us spending the majority of our time in darkened rooms, shutters pulled heavy across glassless windows, sunlight only smattering in through their diamond-shaped holes.

Alexis wanders out to the balcony. He waves his hand over the potted herbs, pinching the lemon balm between his fingers, releasing the scent. And then he puts his hands on the breeze blocks and stares down to the street below. He is not judging the distance. For a long time, I thought that was exactly what he was doing, trying to figure out if he'd die jumping from this height. I never tried to stop him. Figured it was one of those things that he would either do, or not do. But one time, more out of curiosity than anything else, I followed him out. And as I stood beside him, he nodded down at a woman entering the apartment block opposite. In her arms a basket with bread and fruit and parceled meats.

"She's getting home safe," he said. He turned to me then, and smiled to let me know he was happy about that, about life going on while we holed ourselves up in darkness, that out in the world, on the streets below, people were getting home safe. It seemed to make it okay for our own lives to be stalled, stuck in these new-dark rooms, escaping life, escaping the part of it that 'moved on'.

The blast was enough to shake the ground two streets away. But we weren't two streets away.

The thing I remember is the silence. How for that moment, there was a vacuum and it was so great that all the sound of the world was sucked into it. And even after the noise of the day came back, it was muted, our ears made empty by what we'd heard.

We slept in the same bed for the first three days. There was no real waking. We barely moved. At one point, Alexis made me sit up to drink a glass of water. I sipped at the cool and felt it run down inside me. It seemed strange to me, to have a body that was capable of experiencing such sensation when what I thought I felt was numb. We were still in the clothes we'd been wearing. I buried my face in Alexis' back, coating myself in the pale dust that clung to his shirt. Not all dust from the street. It was dust from up there, too. The building. We don't sleep in the same bed anymore. Alexis sleeps on the floor. I have his bed. I often think about how my mother must have slept in this bed, too. My mother was a beautiful woman, more so after we came here to live under the sun. Alexis must have been very much in love with her. And now she's gone, and in a flash, like some wrong magic trick. And he's left with me, sprawled out on his covers, a part of my mother but not her.

We read and we stay quiet. We are still almost strangers. My mother had only just introduced him to us, to me and Clara. And I had taken his hand and shook it, and he was gentle. And all Clara wanted was to go up to the roof. Alexis had interrupted our plans. She wouldn't take his hand. I kissed her head and told her we would go up later. She started to protest, the new gap between her teeth making every word a whistle. The missing tooth she held tight in her fist. I knew then that she wouldn't throw it lightly, knew she was all set to pitch it far into the sky, as if the wish would only stick if the tooth hit the sun. My mother suggested ice cream then, an appeasement. Alexis offered to go and get it. I was volunteered to help. Every day I think, what if I hadn't gone? Or what if we'd all gone? I don't know that I prefer the outcome where I am still here, alive. He hasn't said as much, but I don't know that Alexis does either.

I haven't left this apartment since Alexis brought me here. He ventures out every few days to get food for us, and to pick up the papers and see what's happening in the world. I don't miss the feel of sunlight on my skin. I don't miss the dust that's everywhere outside, or the way it got into my throat and eyes. And I don't miss people. The only people that mattered are gone. No one else has anything to offer me, not even Alexis. I think we're here to keep each other going, but neither of us has figured out quite what for yet. My mother has been dead for seven weeks and two days. My sister, too. And I have been here for all that time. And Alexis has been here. And we have eaten bread and figs and cheese and olives. And we have listened to the radio, the same station my mother always listened to. The one that seemed to be trapped in time, with all the old songs my mother loved so much, the ones with bassoon, clarinet, trumpet, piano. There are certain songs that make us stop. Songs that freeze us where we stand, and all we can do is be still, and listen, and remember my mother, her body warm, moving through the notes and our days, the mundanity and magic of it all.

Both of us, Alexis and I, know I can't stay here forever. There is the need for school. I have aunts who would take me in, set my life back on the appropriate track. But for now, nobody knows I am alive. And sometimes I think that maybe I am dead, maybe Alexis and I died also, only we are in limbo, stuck forever or for a time in these dark rooms, our movements slow, treacle-held, that we died in the street, or we never were in the street, or we made it back to the building. I have toyed with all these possibilities, and none of them seem far-fetched. Maybe this place is a kind of heaven. I have never felt so free.

Alexis stands in the door frame, holding the sun at bay. Still, it pushes through from behind his shoulders and makes a shadow of him on the wall. He is younger than my mother. He reaches out to take a fig from the table. He takes care not to touch me. Those first three days, we held each other and pressed our faces into chests, shoulder blades, arms, bellies. His hands stroked my hair, slid tears across my cheeks. And our bodies lay the whole length of each other, needing to meet, needing to know the other was there. I fused myself into his back. He curled himself around me. And then one day he left the room. And when he came back, there was an unspoken thing with him. And from then on, he made his bed on the floor.

I have never kissed a boy. I have never been kissed. This will change for me, but my sister Clara will never experience these things. My sister Clara no longer exists, except in my memory. Alexis didn't know her. All he has of her is a child wanting to throw her milk tooth into the sky, and refusing to acknowledge him because he has interrupted her plans. He couldn't have known about the tooth, either. So all he knows of her is she didn't want to talk to him. It's awkward meeting people for the first time. I know this. That his last meeting with my mother was tinged with such awkwardness makes me sad. If he'd arrived half an hour later, Clara, tooth-thrown, wish made, would have been back to her friendly, eager to please self. She would have hugged his legs and made him feel he had always belonged. I wonder what she would have wished for? Probably madeleines. Or a kitten. She wouldn't have known to wish for 'no bomb'. Would a wish have covered it anyway? These things have a way of happening under their own steam. People who are powerful have their own plans for things.

I sink my teeth into the fig. My tongue tastes sweetness, sharpness. Alexis peels his fig and bites into it. The air inside these rooms is so still. It makes me always on the point of sleep. The way my body moves now is slow and lazy. There is nothing to run to, or from. I feel like my limbs are trapped in a dance that is all time-lapse, as I move from one room to the other. The sun catches the hairs on Alexis' arm and they glow. He never looks me in the eye, except for when he's speaking. And then he holds my gaze as if blinking just once could vanish the world away. He mumbles to himself in his own language, too, mostly at night. Sometimes he'll wake me with a sharp cry. But I don't understand his vowels. These exchanges are lost on me. I know we can't stay this way forever. But he hasn't said anything about me leaving yet. And I'm not ready to go anyway. I like this not existing.

The song on the radio becomes one that my mother would dance to, with arms rising and falling through the air, legs kicked out, whole body twirling. She would take the blanket from the back of the sofa and wrap it around her body, and then twist, revealing a leg raised, an arm taut against the blanket's edge. I get to my feet. My limbs are heavy. I lift my arms out to the side and let my fingers rest in the space between ceiling and floor, pulling at imaginary strings. And then I tilt, and one arm stretches to the ceiling. I turn on this axis. My body flows through the motion. It hasn't forgotten the shapes my mother imprinted on me. She could be here, in the room, guiding my feet, holding my arms strong and loose. Alexis watches me. He is anchored to the wall. His arms are pressed flat against the cool of the plaster. I spin. I hear trumpet. I hear piano. I spin. I am my mother, balancing the tightrope across our lives. I am barefoot, and the clothes I have on are the only clothes I have that are mine. The last part of my old life that's left. Alexis is still at the wall. He hasn't blinked for the entirety of this song. I spin. I am the shapes of my mother. My hair hangs loose across my shoulders, falls into my eyes, obscures my face. This body is a gift. This body knows loss, and yet it can still move like this, my feet pointing, lifting to the sky, and the rest of me turning and twirling. And my arms. I spin. And my breathing is deep. The air in here is too still. Too heavy. And Alexis is quiet and breathing slowly, behind him the balcony and the sun and all that air. I spin. The song is loud at my back. All of the trumpets and cornets and the French horns. I jump. I run. I hit into Alexis in the doorway. He stumbles backwards,

knocking the herb pots to the floor, but blocks my path. I try
to keep moving and his arms fold around me. Still I run, shove.
I am my mother and I am me and I need to breathe air that is
light, that is not full of darkness. I push against his body but
Alexis doesn't move. His hands are on me, holding me fast. My
mouth is open on his shirt, half scream, half kiss. I breathe, but I
don't move away.

The song ends. I don't recognise the next one. I breathe in
Alexis: fresh sweat, sandalwood, coffee. My mouth is open on his
shirt and I won't scream now. I let my tongue touch the fabric. I
move my mouth slow.

Alexis relaxes his grip and leans away from me. We have
grown used to communicating without words. I know already
what this means.

I step out onto the balcony. The soil has spilled out from
the herb pots. It looks like cake crumbs. One of the pots has
smashed. Tiny strings of thyme lie on the floor. I bend to scoop
the soil up in my hands, and I see the porcelain fragments glint-
ing white.

There is no tooth fairy here. Children throw their fallen milk
teeth up into the sky, and in exchange, they get a wish. I pick a
piece of the broken pot out of the soil, a small piece. It could be
a tooth. I hold it in my fist. I hold it tight. And then I throw it as
hard and as high as I can.

The Devil's Hands
Annabel Banks

It had happened again. Two in one night, this time, and the whole pub was a-buzzing with talk of Berner Street. The sailors in the far corner, tired whores perched on their knees; the toffs, with their good beer and giggles, scarves wrapped so high around their faces that only the tips of fat noses could be seen, pink with drink and their own daring. As if we cared who they were. Nothing but a holiday for them, you see. Just a ghost story to give chills before bed, sleeping safe and warm in their fine houses, glutted on the horror of other people's deaths.

But listen to me. What a fraud I am.

In our group Old Mack was the loudest, his cup slopping as he shouted the odds, forgetting how him and me earn our bread and beer. Still, a girl and her master have to eat, and it's a fact that the fairground on Whitechapel Road has picked up a treat since the whispers started. We all know it. The crowds come for a gossip and a peek, or a hard stare into the face of a street girl, as if their eyes could cut. Urchins offer tours for a coin, and if that's not enough… well, that's where me and Mack come in.

Our newest exhibition is called Murder Most Foul. Posed Tragedy In Wax. Personal tours available, and nothing more than that, despite what some might think. You shouldn't listen to rumours. They only send you wrong. And never mind that each murder meant such a scramble for me. No time to wire mould, cast in plaster. No time to do it right. "We need the shock to bring the shillings," Mack had said. "Just take any old figure and do your best." So I did.

The fire smoked and smouldered as we'd sat around it, our boots cracking in the heat, while soot from the blocked chimney collected on our tongues. The talk turned to the girls themselves, sorrows and sins, and the men got so excited, all red faced and righteous, with frothing white flecks in the corners of their mouths. Dollymops get this reaction from the worst sort of man; they call them filth and dirt and nothing until it's after closing and they still have a penny or two weighing in their grimy purses. I don't think like that. I know what it's like not to have what you need to warm you, in whatever way you need to be warmed. We know the names, even if we don't know the girls. We all know a Polly. We all know a Liz. And if now they're saying Kate was no whore: well, much good it did her.

It didn't take long for the Mister Brooks to come over and join the tales, leaving his missus to tend bar on her own. He was all a-flutter with talk of cutting. Told us how he knew that poor Annie, or said he did, at least. You can't spit on Whitechapel Road without hitting someone who knew the girls well, willing to give you their theories and opinions, if you have an hour or three to spare. Seems to me the girls could have used more friends when they were alive. But that's just my sympathy talking. And, as I'm to make money from their deaths, what is such sympathy worth?

As the talk got louder and bloodier I pulled my jacket close around my throat. I wasn't cold, for we were lucky to be close to the heat on this chill autumn night, but I shivered none the less as I listened to old Mack hold court, all proud over his professional interest in the case.

"You don't sculpt the faces," he said. "But we'll have to for this work. It's an art to get it red and ragged."

Hark at him. As if he did any of the delicate stuff. He's only fit for painting background scenes and shouting up customers. It's why he took me on. I had my training in the back room of the best funeral parlour in Hounslow, and the Misters were sad to lose me, I'll have you know. The faces of the departed are blue and yellow, not white, not wax. I spent three years learning how to hide the marks of death on sunken flesh, and when the loved ones came in, to cry and wail and pay their debt, they expected to see their money well spent. They wanted their dead restored to an image of life, carrying off colours they hadn't worn for years. And I could do it. Fine brushes and a light touch, wire, putty and cotton swabs. Painting moulded wax is easier, of course; you can't melt the faces of the dead into shape. Wigs and paper help, and bright glass eyes. Mack's little boy cries for them to put in his mouth. Sometimes I let him, just to keep him quiet, even though it looks so wrong.

As the talk rolled through the smoke I started planning how to render the women in wax. The figures waited in the work-shop, silent and hopeful, one dress and a paper crown away from becoming Queen Elizabeth, or even Her Majesty herself. That's what I like the best: a bit of glamour for the gawpers. My wax-works have brought the finest nobs into the Pyle, even if it was just their images for me to dress up, playing with my huge dolls. I always thought we should show the very best of the world, using metal's strong frame, the beehive's waxen gift. Not the worst: never poor whores cut by the blade of a madman.

Before I knew it, I'd said so. The beer must have been stronger than I'd thought, because I'd spoken too loudly and caused a hush. Faces turned to me and I had to go on, to explain myself, even though I was sore at heart. I did so, opening my hands and looking down into them.

"And pity me, who has to rush the work. No time to even cast

34

a wound. I'll have to cut the faces myself. Not looking forward to that bit of business, am I?"

"Why's that?" Some market man fingered my knee. "Scared to get it wrong?"

My colour was rising. "You'll think me foolish."

They pressed me, and as I looked around the dark room, at the glittering eyes, I thought of the master's boy. The eye in his mouth. "I feel... I fear some of the sin will be sent my way. For repeating the crime."

Mack tapped the toe of my boot with his own. "Didn't know you for such a soft one." He leaned back and yawned, teeth as brown as river water. "I'll have to dock your wages, girlie."

"Such as they are." I scowled at him, but he just raised his glass to my troubles. The talk went on but I'd made myself sober, and stayed silent as the logs popped and sparked. First thing tomorrow, I vowed, I'll finish the figures, and we can open the doors to the panting crowds. And I will take the coins, hand them to Mack, and trust the wax to seal the whole bloody mess into the past.

There's no one asleep on the waxhouse steps this morning, which has less do with the cold, I'd wager, than the Whitechapel murders. This is what we call them now. I hurry to unlock the door and light the lamp. It is very early: sunrise more than an hour away, but my sleep had been troubled. No corpse I'd dressed had ever entered my dreams, however violently their lives had ended, but the smooth, blank faces of my poor dollies kept looming from my mind's shadows and prevented my rest. I need to get this done.

Sorting clothes from the pile in the small storeroom, I make sure they are as ruined as they should be, with missing buttons and many a stain. The customers will be looking for bosom and leg, but these women dress for warmth, layers of cloth hiding their wares until they can find a dry place to pull their skirts up. Doll Polly's dress was in a lot bought from the bailiff, rags and clothing taken for debt, lost for drink and tobacco. At the bottom of the sack was a pair of tiny shoes, that of a child's. Somewhere a little one has to walk its new, soft flesh against stone. It's enough to make you weep, to grab a knife and start slashing at things yourself, but it wouldn't change anything. Not here. Not now.

The dresses I choose are black and dirty, but with faded white frills that go across the chest and behind the bodice buttons. I'll rip them open with the tip of my scissors and fill bladders with paint to stab and cut at, and it will show up well enough. They won't have to look too hard to fill their eyes with red, though I can't stop it drying. They'll have to provide their own wetness, whether through tears or something nastier, I'm loathe to guess.

Figures dressed and headless, I take the first wax head and begin. The softness is still surprising to my fingers, after years of manipulating the immobile dead. It curves under the pressure of a thumb, Mack's own recipe. "Something for you to inherit," he'll wheeze now and again, as if I'd want to. Slowly, with finger and blade, I follow the curve of wax masks over wire skulls, padded with cotton cheekbones, and make the adjustments. Tricks of the trade. Trades. I cut a throat, and poor Liz is done.

Kate's turn. I wonder whether to give her eyes open or closed. Open means I must find out the colour of her eyes, but closed will give the appearance of peace, and that's not what the waxwork is for. She must have seen the blade being pulled out. I pull out my own, and pause, and although it's been many a year since I saw the inside of a church I find the words on my tongue, something about heaven and forgiveness.

I hear a tread on the step. I hear the door open.

I colour her cheekbone and add the eyebrows. They said her face was mutilated, proper messed up, so I have to decide what to do. Should I close my own eyes and make some wild cuts? I could stand on the clothing box, to add the inches needed. I could hold my breath. But what if I go too deep, or pull at the gentle fringe of eyelash, pulling it away? It takes an age to position that line of hair. What if, when I open my eyes, blood is seeping out of the wax?

I'm scaring myself now. A soft one, Mack called me, and that's right. Not tender, but soft in the head. All the time working with the actual dead, all through the night sometimes, and never a shake in my heart; I won't let myself be frightened. Not now. Not when there's nothing here.

Someone is behind me. I can hear his breath. Why not turn around, to taunt Mack that his wife has locked him out again?

I know why.

I hear a sound, metal and cloth, and a blade appears over my shoulder. The oil lamp flares and I see the rest of the room, the waxes, the clothes, the box of eyes staring blindly, but with more knowledge than I have of what is happening. I can't hear his breath any more, because my heart is in my ears and the thud, thud, thud of my life's beat drowns it out.

The blade continues forward and his hand comes into view. I can't tell you about this hand. We make a silent bargain, him and me, in these cold seconds, and if I break my side of it I'll see those hands again, that's for sure. So I won't tell you about its age, or the rings it may wear, wedding or signet; the roughened texture of a labouring man; the smooth white padding of a toff. I can't tell you. Don't ask me to.

As the blade moves up and down before my eyes, I feel his other hand take my shoulder, the fingers grip, gently, so gently, the back of my neck, and I know not to turn. There is a smell... something new to me. If silk flowers gave a scent it would mayhap be this, sweet, but unnatural; a warning touch of wrong-ness. He begins to cut, and I hear the soft sound of his lips parting, because he smiles as he works.

One cut over the eyelid. One cut down the cheek. And another. And again.

When the tip of her nose comes off I take a breath in. I can't help it: a reaching, shuddering breath that whines and squeals over my closed throat. I want to cough. I want to turn. I will turn, and surely be damned, left on the floor for the master's boy to find: a welcoming smile carved into my throat, a blind eye peeping from my silenced mouth.

The grip on the knife tightens, but it's those fingers on my flesh that hold me still. They squeeze, hard, and again I make a small noise, a child's whimper. I don't want to: I want to be made of silent wood, of uncuttable stone, but this tiny whine escapes me and I bite my inside lip till it bleeds. Under my skirts, my knees are shaking properly now, the thigh muscles aching as if I held his weight up as well as my own, and I know that any moment I will fall.

Blade moves back. Pressure is gone. Lips seek my ear.

Shh.

The door closes, and I concentrate on the footfalls, the firm step moving away, into the distant stirring of the street.

I'll tell no one. The police never come to the waxworks, so no one will ask about the cuts. I won't go back to the pub, to look around at those who hold drinks, clutch pipes, scratch at heads. Instead, I'll lock the door, and sleep with my own hands over my mouth.

Yes, you've got questions.

But I've already said too much.

Time Gentlemen Please
William Gallagher

I was ready to turn this corner, wait by this door, to see my younger self come through as I had come through it before. The reality of standing here wasn't all that much different from the years of imagining it.

This side of the simple toilet door, my side of the door, the Gents. An ordinary, typical, boring Gents toilet, an outer door to the bar, this inner door into the toilets. Empty then, empty now but for me.

That side, well. Back then, back when I was first here, when I was that young and it was this same night, I thought it was a glorious time. I'd say that I had been thinking only of rushing back out and being with my new friends. But in truth I hadn't thought at all, too excited.

Too full of her.

Now will be different. My younger self will come through that door any moment and I am going to stop me. Just put my hand on his chest and say "Please". I wondered if my younger self would understand, I wanted him to be clever enough to understand, but it doesn't matter. If I confuse him, if I scare him, it doesn't matter, just delay him here for one minute, stop him going out when he went out before.

Just one minute. A few seconds.

Maybe you can always time travel when you know this, when

you know to the minute, to the second when it all went wrong, so badly wrong; outside this room, through that door, the things said and not said, the things I've done that I couldn't ever undo.

Until now.

Now I can undo them, now I can stop myself ever doing them. Just a quiet word and if I listen, great. If I don't, fine. I delay him and everything will be fine.

I was ready to see myself.

The door moved. The outside door was being opened. My younger self was out there opening it and the air bumped the inner door. I felt a pressure on my chest, nerves and excitement and a little fear pushing in on me.

Right where I planned to place my hand on him.

I looked down.

Someone else's hand was on my chest.

Because I was standing next to me. An older me is standing next to me.

I looked substantially older and not very well. But the person staring at me from a cubicle doorway had the same expression I was planning to use, serious, calming, sober, strong.

He looked at me as the gents door swung open and my younger self came in.

"Please," said the older me in the cubicle.

He moved his hand from my chest to my arm. It was still only a little touch, a little pressure, but it was commanding and I stepped inside with him.

He closed the cubicle door. Raised a finger to his lips.

And we waited for me to leave.

Glazed Eyes
Brian Ennis

He awoke that morning in another man's bed, entangled with
another man's wife. She begged him to stay, but he couldn't;
to stay was to invite scrutiny and that way lay the hangman's
noose. She settled for quizzing him over breakfast, probing for
his secrets, questioning why he wasn't performing for kings and
queens rather than travelling the countryside in a rickety wooden
cart. He told her that he had sold his soul to the devil in order to
be the best entertainer in all the world, and the travelling life was
God's punishment. She laughed, pleasantly shocked by his blas-
phemy, and fed him another apricot. When she asked his name,
having not bothered in the heat of the night before, he told her
he was the Marionettist - his art was his life, and he was his art.
He never told anyone his real name; there was power in names,
and the profligacy with which others shared theirs shocked him.

He left the village a hero, children running alongside his cart
like sheepdogs, adults cheering and clapping as if his show was
still in progress. It was ever thus; he arrived a curiosity, promis-
ing entertainment, and left a legend. They would speak of him
in whispers for years to come: the power of his performance, his
great dramatic range, and more than anything the grace of his
marionettes, his fingers dextrous on their controls, teasing movements from them that were elegant and almost human. How
he was able to convey such a variety of emotion with wooden

puppets was nothing short of miraculous.

He charted a course for the nearest town, hoping to reach it before nightfall. The village was barely out of sight when a small wooden head poked through the curtain that closed off the cart's interior. Its eyes were glittering beads beneath its extravagantly-plumed helmet, and its hinged jaw moved of its own accord, producing a surprisingly deep voice.

"Sir." It snapped a salute, its hinged arm moving independently, devoid of string. "The troops wish to know our destination."

"Get back in there, you'll be seen." The Marionettist grabbed St George by the face and thrust him back into the cart. "We're going to market. I need materials for our new arrival."

From inside the cart came a clatter, like a week's firewood being dropped down the stairs. "Quiet back there," the Marionettist hissed, "what if someone's followed us? You know the rules."

Another marionette poked its head out, this one wearing a gaudy crown. "Sorry boss," it stage-whispered, louder than most shouts, "we were hoping we could go to the village instead and…"

It shot backwards, cut off mid-sentence. The Milkmaid separated the curtains daintily.

"What the Foolish King meant to say," she said, fluttering her horsehair eyelashes, "is that we were not happy with the performance last night. We would like to try some improvements in front of a smaller audience before a big show at a market town." She fluttered some more. "If you would be so kind, master."

"Bollocks will I. We are going to town, and that's that. Now, all of you, shut up before I string you up."

"Do you need a new apprentice? Villagers are keener to share their children. I remember…"

He pushed her back into the cart.

They rumbled along in blessed silence, the Marionettist

daydreaming about his latest project and what kind of apprentice would suit it best. A crack and a jolt broke his reverie. His donkey brayed in protest and stopped in the road. Swearing, he hopped out and immediately saw the problem: a cartwheel was broken.

Jack Ketch jumped down next to him, collapsing in a boneless heap before straightening up.

"Looks bad," Ketch said, as if the whole matter was hilarious. "We're gonna be stuck here a while."

"Fix it," the Marionettist told him. "All of you!" A dozen marionettes jumped down onto the road.

"You didn't want us to be seen," the Foolish King said, scratching beneath the band of his crown. "Surely you should do it?"

"Hush now, my liege." St George knelt before the King. "We have our creator's orders. It is not our place to question God."

"Of course!" the Foolish King said, as if it had been obvious all along, and moved into place.

"Stand watch," the Marionettist told Punchinello. "Your voice is enough to wake the dead." Punchinello gave a high-pitched cackle and leapt to the top of the cart.

The Marionettist climbed into the cart's cool interior and dozed until Ketch shook him awake.

"We're done," Ketch said. "Won't make the town tonight though. Shame." The paint around his face and hands was badly chipped, and he had grass stains up his legs. The Marionettist sighed; he would have to waste time he could have spent on the new addition tidying Ketch up before the next performance.

The repair looked good, but Ketch was right, it would grow dark soon. The Marionettist's map showed a village a mile or so away, unnamed, marked only with a shaky, hand-drawn cross.

Perhaps the Milkmaid was right; he might find a new apprentice at a village, a callow youth eager to please, easily tricked. It would be pleasing to arrive in town with a new player.

"Looks like you'll get your practice show after all," he said, and urged his donkey on.

The Marionettist was used to arriving at a new town or village with a fanfare, children calling out requests for their favourite stories, women in windows watching him pass, village elders competing for the honour of housing him beneath their roof.

This village was different.

It was so small as to be churchless, a true rarity, its godless-ness seemingly punished with abject poverty. Hovels lined its single pitiful road, roof beams bowed and collapsing under rotten thatches, walls stained yellow and brown like smokers' teeth. At first he thought the village was deserted but, in amongst the animal pens, he spotted children, gaunt and hollow-eyed, staring at his passing as blankly as the cows and sheep in whose excre-ment they squatted. None ran to join him.

At its centre an ancient stone fountain thrust up from the ground at a drunken angle, topped with a worn and faceless cherub, its fingers crumbled to ineffectual stubs, its bulbous wings more like cancerous growths than delicate instruments of flight. Beneath it a brass plaque hung on for grim life, whatever words once written there long eroded.

A group of locals came to meet him, four men carrying tools, fresh from tilling the lifeless local fields, and two women dressed in long puritanical dresses that fastened tight around the neck and hung down shapelessly, tattered hems scuffing the ground with every step.

The Marionettist smiled and opened his arms. "Good evening!" he cried. "I hereby invite you all to attend the great-est puppet show you will ever see. In exchange, I ask only room, board, and a hot meal."

The six villagers watched him, saying nothing. He grinned at

44

them until it hurt, suddenly aware of the damage a well-swung hoe or scythe could do to a human body. Eventually one of the women stepped forward, the movement so unexpected as to make him flinch. She looked familiar, but then again, the hard life of a peasant woman ground them down until they all looked the same. She gestured for him to follow.

The Marionettist shivered. He should leave, sleep in the cart and set the marionettes to watch out for thieves and bandits. A night at risk of murder would surely be better than whatever this God-forsaken place could muster in the way of hospitality. Of course, if he tried to flee they might take exception to his rudeness.

He had no choice but to follow her to a ramshackle barn. The stench of rotting straw and rat shit was thick enough to make his eyes water, and the donkey had to be thoroughly whipped to force it inside. The peasant woman left without a word, and he wedged the door shut behind her with a block of wood.

"Is she gone?" Ketch called out.

"Hush yourself!" the Marionettist hissed. The donkey brayed with fear. "They may be stupid, but they're not deaf."

The marionettes tumbled out of the cart. "I like it here," the Foolish King decreed, to which Punchinello blew a raspberry. St George chased the Dragon while the Milkmaid smoothed out her skirts, watched by a pair of sombre cardinals in dusty robes.

"Get the stage up quickly," he said. They looked at him, their glazed eyes so like the villagers' that he lost his line of thought for a moment. "The sooner we perform, the sooner we can leave."

"I still like it here," the Foolish King grumbled. "The people seem nice."

While the marionettes assembled the wooden stage the Marionettist climbed into the back of the cart. Jack Ketch had laid out the parts of an unfinished marionette, its base wood raw, grainy and unsanded, its limbs lying in a separate heap.

"Nearly ready?" Ketch asked.

"So close, yet so far," the Marionettist replied. "We won't be picking up an apprentice here, that's for certain."

"Perhaps a girl, from town?" The Marionettist had done it before, but it was far riskier taking girls, and no one gave him any money for them.

"Perhaps," he said. "Now go and help. There's something wrong about this place."

"Bit unnatural, ain't it?" Ketch twisted his hangman's rope in his wooden hands like he was wringing its neck, and laughed.

The marionettes had the stage up and lit in double time. They were unusually excited, stage-whispering amongst themselves and causing a racket, and he had to hush them several times before he could throw open the barn doors.

Outside a couple of dozen villagers huddled together, like sheep in winter. They turned their heads to him as one, and he shivered.

"Come, one and all," the Marionettist cried. "Come and be entertained!"

He retreated behind the stage. The crowd filed in and sat down in the muck, oblivious to the filth. No one spoke.

He whispered his commands and the performance began, the marionettes leaping and dancing beneath his hands, the strings giving the illusion that they were normal puppets. He started with a satire; the lower the man, the more joy he took in scorning his betters, and these villagers looked to be the lowest of the low. The Foolish King performed admirably as an idiot ruler repeatedly changing his faith for political gain, in fine comic form.

No one laughed.

No one moved.

No one spoke a word.

Perhaps the women's puritan dresses indicated godliness: in his experience the godly rarely laughed. He hissed his orders and the players and scenery changed to tell the tale of Jonah and the Whale.

The villagers watched on like an unwilling congregation enduring a terrible sermon for the sake of their souls.

Perhaps this was all too intellectual. He changed tack again, sending out the Old Man and the Milkmaid to perform a crude, lecherous comedy. One boy, caked in mud and what looked suspiciously like shit, poked a finger into a nostril and began to root around.

Otherwise, nothing.

Cold panic sweat dripped down the Marionettist's back. He tried another tale, and another, and another. Punchinello failed to amuse them, as did St George and the Dragon, Three Blind Mice, and the Song of Roland. Soon all the marionettes were out, either on stage or lying behind the curtain, staring at him as if this was his fault.

Soaked through, arms aching from the pretence of performance, he stopped.

Nothing. No reaction, no applause, not even a boo or a hiss.

He stepped out from behind the curtain and gave a stiff, awkward bow.

The crowd rose as one, as if in standing ovation, but there was no pleasure in their eyes. Still bowed, he peered up at them.

Still expressionless, they charged.

Sudden desperation made him flee to the back of the barn. He threw himself against the back door, its rusted hinges shrieking in protest. The crowd moved in, slow but unstoppable, and seized him, their ragged nails clawing his flesh as they dragged him to the ground.

They beat him as they had watched his show: silent, sombre, as if performing a necessary but immeasurably dull chore. The only sounds were their grunts of exertion, the Marionettist's cries, and the braying of his fearful donkey.

The beating stopped as suddenly as it began. Through a forest of legs he saw his creations, his beautiful children, pulling themselves from the wreckage of the stage. "Help me!" he cried out to them. "Help me!"

The crowd parted, leaving a clear path through the fetid hay for his marionettes to follow. Jack Ketch led the way, skipping and swinging his hangman's noose, followed by the Milkmaid, Punchinello, and the rest. The Foolish King looked around and asked what was happening; the others shushed him. The villagers reacted to living, talking puppets the way they reacted to everything, with dull disinterest, like cows watching a massacre.

"Help me," the Marionettist whispered.

Ketch shook his head. He slipped his noose over the Marionettist's head, and pulled.

The world turned red and black as he was dragged through the filth and out into the centre of the village. Candles had been laid in the grass, lighting up the drunken fountain and the hideous, deformed cherub. More rope was looped around his wrists and ankles. Following Ketch's orders, the villagers hauled him up to hang from the fountain. St George waved his little wooden sword like a conductor's baton, directing the villagers to pull him this way and that, twisting him into unnatural shapes that tore and dislocated his joints. He didn't have the breath to scream.

An eternity later they stopped, leaving him crucified against the cherub's wings, arms outstretched, the noose around his neck loosened just enough to allow him to breathe.

"Why?" the Marionettist sobbed.

Jack Ketch climbed up to sit on the Marionettist's shoulder. "We yearn," Ketch said. "We yearn for flesh."

"Why are these bastards helping you? What have I ever done to them and their God-forsaken village?"

"For the dispossessed, the flesh yearns for spirit." Ketch shrugged. "We have what they lack, too. An ideal match, don't ya think?"

"I never knew. I thought you were happy, I swear."

The marionettes laughed.

"You think we want this?" Ketch said, and rapped his head with his wooden fist. "That we wish to be cold and unfeeling, while you revel in earthly pleasures?"

"I wanted you to be my children." The Marionettist swallowed; talking hurt. "Forever."

"Undo it, you bastard."

The Marionettist nodded as best he could. "I need the book."

Punchinello and his wife scampered off. They returned carrying a worn and cracked leather-bound tome, its cover emblazoned with a two-headed crow, wings spread wide. It took both of them to open it.

"Tell me how," Ketch demanded.

"Let me down and I will," the Marionettist said.

St George waved his sword again and the villagers hauled on the ropes, sending fresh waves of agony through the Marionettist's wracked body.

"We don't dance to your tune anymore," St George declared. "You dance for us now."

"I'm sorry," the Marionettist whimpered.

"Tell me, Gregor," Ketch said.

The Marionettist had thought it impossible to be any more terrified, but he had been wrong. "How do you know my name?"

Ketch's dull eyes glimmered black in the moonlight. "Is it so strange for a child to know the name of God?"

Once Gregor had whispered all his secrets to Ketch he was released, crashing into the brackish water at the base of the fountain. Two villagers hauled him out before he could drown and dumped him in the mud. They were, he thought, either heroes for saving his life or monsters for prolonging his suffering.

The marionettes formed a circle, while the villagers gathered round and watched, dead-eyed, like sheep clustering for warmth. They read together from the book, voices growing louder and louder. The Milkmaid led a villager into the centre of the circle: the woman who had shown Gregor to the barn. The villager knelt and the Milkmaid reached up a wooden hand to caress her cheek.

Twenty years had passed but the Marionettist had never forgotten the smile that now bloomed on the villager's face, a smile that had once belonged to a child, a child he had abandoned, standing empty on the side of the road. So, this was where they went, the empty vessels he and his kind left behind.

He knew then that there would be no mercy.

The marionettes began to chant, repeating the Milkmaid's name, her real name, the name of the girl she had once been. The Milkmaid collapsed to the floor and the chanting stopped.

The woman blinked and looked around her, as if waking from sleepwalking. That grin spread across her face once more and she looked suddenly alive, as if some vital missing component had been restored. "It worked!" she cried, in the Milkmaid's voice. The voices rose again. In turn, each marionette picked a villager and led them into the circle, like children eager to show off something new.

One by one, the marionettes fell, lifeless, to the floor.

One by one, the villagers straightened, blinked, gazed around. And smiled.

Soon, only the Foolish King remained. "I'm happy as I am!" he cried, and raced off. They let him go.

The girl who had been Jack Ketch stood over the Marionettist. "As for you," she said, her new eyes glittering, "you're not the only one who can be creative."

The next day the Foolish King, resplendent in his wooden sovereignty, stood atop the fountain to wave the others off, the remaining villagers forming a silent, hollow-eyed guard of honour. A dozen men and women sat on or followed the cart, their movements clumsy, still adjusting to their new forms. Jack Ketch, always good with ropes, took the reins. That so many villagers remained meant that there were more troupes out there, more blasphemies to be undone.

One villager, however, would always remain.

"Gee up, Gregor," she cried. The donkey brayed and twisted its head; a quick lash from Ketch's switch chastened him, and he led them out into the sunshine, dragging his burden behind him.

Gregor's old form watched them go, eyes glazed.

Lost and Found
Richard Farren Barber

Michael eased down on the brake to slow the car further still. The needle of the speedometer wavered around the twenty mph mark and when he glanced in the rear view mirror the line of following cars trailed off into infinity.

"We need to find the perfect spot," he said under his breath. Beside him, Bess was silent.

The car behind blasted its horn – long and low like a Canadian Pacific train. Michael shrugged and blanked out the sound.

"No time to be rushed," he murmured. He looked down at the speedometer and feathered the brake again. Through a clump of trees he spotted an empty parking area, but the entrance drifted past while he was still deciding whether to stop.

"Maybe the perfect spot doesn't exist," Bess said.

"Of course it does," Michael said, even though the same thought had occurred to him, "it has to exist."

The road crested a hill and dropped down into a valley. There was a small village nested in a fold of green fields where flecks of white dotted the landscape, as if someone had carefully placed each sheep and cow onto the canvas.

A hundred yards ahead a large blue 'P' sign signalled a lay-by.

"This is it," Michael said and clicked on the indicator. The metallic noise filled the car.

Bess didn't sigh. He had to give her that. She was patient. When they stopped he leaned across and pecked her on the cheek to say thank you.

They sat for a moment, listening to the ticking of the cooling engine and waiting for the stream of traffic to pass. He needed to see this landscape properly, to hold it in his mind and remember it.

Bess moved first. She unclipped her seat belt and reached back for the large gingham shopping bag. It always reminded Michael of Sunday afternoon drives. The bag couldn't be more than a year old and yet it was part of an unbroken tradition that stretched back decades. When the hessian began to unravel the bag would miraculously be replaced with another; the new blue deeper than the Med, the white as bright as a washing powder advert. Sometimes he considered asking Bess where they came from, but it was part of the magic.

He checked over his shoulder and once the road was clear he opened the door and stepped out onto the carriageway. Quickly he opened the boot to retrieve the two folding chairs. He positioned them at the back of the car to look down the valley.

"Perfect." Bess put the gingham bag down between the two chairs.

Michael smiled. "Yes, it is, isn't it?" The lay-by was empty. Just as it should be. He paused for a moment. The air tasted of diesel and exhaust fumes. There was no traffic on the road, but the low rumble from the other side of the hill suggested that this would soon change. But here, now, this was heaven.

Bess took the rug out and placed it across her knees while Michael took out the flask of coffee and poured two cups. They bumped the rims together and Bess whispered, "Clink." Michael smiled. It was the rituals that made the picnic so important. Small things like finding the right place to park and passing out the sandwiches from the Tupperware container in just the right order: one for him, one for Bess, one for him, and Bess's habit of pretending they were sipping champagne on the banks of the

Seine rather than coffee on the side of the A57. All of this was important.

"Do you want a custard cream?" Michael asked. The packet wavered in the air between them. He looked into her wide eyes and tried to guess what was on her mind.

"No thanks," Bess said.

He ate his sandwiches from the inside out, burrowing through the bread like a worm. When they were first married Bess had packed them in tin foil and cut away the crusts. Some days he would find a small hand-written note in with his lunch, or maybe just a drawing of a love heart or 'Bess 4 Michael'. He didn't remember when the notes had stopped. He didn't remember when the crusts had stayed on the bread.

But that was life. It didn't mean she loved him any less, just as the way they now sat at the side of the road in silence didn't mean he was no longer interested in what she had to say. They were comfortable together, that was what mattered.

He dropped the dry crusts back into the Tupperware box and snapped shut the lid. The thick wet ham coated his tongue. He tried to swallow but it didn't make any difference. All he could taste was dead pig.

The food reminded him of the first time he knew he loved Bess. They'd been together for months and more than once he'd considered breaking off the relationship because there was nothing there. No spark. They'd been at a party; some godawful thing organised by a colleague from work, where he was expected to laugh at the boss's jokes and make small talk with Matthew from accounts who only spoke about the Triumph motorcycle he was going to buy one day.

Bess had been trapped in the corner with the boor from stock control, an ugly man with terrible body odour and a habit of standing too close. Michael stepped away to the kitchen for a moment and on his return he found Bess in a state of near panic.

"I thought you were gone," she told him.

He handed her a plastic tumbler filled with warm Liebfraumilch. "I'll never leave you," he told her. "Never." The passion behind the words surprised him as much as they did her.

At the side of the road, Michael took a drink of bitter coffee and the plastic taste lingered in his mouth long after the heat had faded. He huddled deeper into the chair. The metal struts creaked under the weight of his body.

"What are you thinking about?" Bess asked.

"Sheep." He watched the small tufts of white to make the lie into a truth.

"What about them?"

He tried to catch sight of her from the corner of his eye, but Bess had moved behind him so that all he could see was the road stretching down into the valley.

"They don't care, do they? About anything. They just stand in the heat or the cold or the rain and they eat and that's all they do and then the farmer ships them off to the abattoir and they're gone, but none of the other sheep notice and they don't care."

It was the longest speech he could remember making for many years. He heard Bess take a slurp from her mug. When Bess leaned forward to pick up the empty plastic mugs he told her, "I haven't finished yet." From the corner of his eye he noticed her startled expression. Just for a moment a fleeting look on her face revealed that he had surprised her.

"But there's nothing left to eat," Bess said.

He was about to answer when a truck blasted past. The metal side of the lorry was close enough to touch. The passage of the truck battered the air around him, whipping it into a storm of grit and exhaust fumes and when Michael opened his eyes the truck was gone.

And so was Bess.

Panic flared in him. She can't leave me. He rose and for a

second the image of the two empty chairs struck him as so significant that he stood there frozen, staring down at the canvas seats. The paralysis lasted only a moment and then Michael whirled around in search of his wife.

"Bess?" he called. He stepped toward the car and had the absurd notion that she was engaged in an impromptu game of hide and seek. He would find her curled in the foot well of the passenger seat or lying across the back of the car. He hurried to check, and when he found the car empty the stillness and silence of the vehicle heightened his tension.

The ground around the empty chairs was littered with the remains of their lunch; plastic plates and knives, the Tupperware box with his guilty crusts inside like artefacts from a museum, the type of place he would drag Bess around with the promise of coffee and a cake in the café afterwards.

He staggered away from the car and stomped across the litter-strewn verge calling her name.

"Bess? Beth? Elizabeth?"

She hated her full name. He shouted again, looking for a reaction. "Elizabeth. We need to get back. It will be dark soon."

He looked up to the sky, white as new steel.

The road was empty and he stepped onto the grey tarmac and looked from one end of the lay-by to the other. There was no place for her to hide.

A caravan pulled into the space behind the empty chairs. Michael hurried to pick up the debris from his picnic; the Tupperware containers and orange peel and empty flask snatched into a plastic carrier bag before the driver of the caravan could get out of her seat.

Michael hesitated before opening the boot of the car. He checked behind him, but the woman was still far away so he stuffed the bag of rubbish down the side and slammed down the lid before the woman was too close.

She was in her thirties; black hair cut into a tight bob and blue jeans that followed the curve of her thighs. She reminded him of Elizabeth. Elizabeth as she was forty years ago.

He looked away, wondering what she saw when she looked at him, an old man camped alone at the side of a busy road. When she got back into her SUV she would probably lean towards the shadow in the passenger seat and they would share a laugh, because that was all he was now, something for other people to laugh at.

"Are you alright?" she asked.

Have you seen Bess? He nearly asked. The words formed at the back of his throat but he stopped; unable to explain to this stranger that he had lost her. Mislaid her like a set of keys.

She wanted to help. Michael felt the need pulsing off her like heat. They all thought that they could make it better: the nurses, the counsellors, the carers. He wanted to shout at the woman to leave him alone, but instead he stared down the valley, ignoring her.

He watched from the corner of his eye as she stood away from the door and drew down on a cigarette. The perfume of tobacco crossed the gap between them and he could taste it at the back of his throat.

When the woman returned to her vehicle Michael glanced back at the single chair at the side of the road. He stood beside it and waited for the caravan to leave.

Silence returned to the roadside once more. The low grumble of approaching traffic grew in volume, but Michael could still hear the bleating of sheep from the bottom of the valley and the ragged engine of a tractor working the fields. He turned around. The land banked behind him; the lay-by cut from the side of the mountain. Bess had left. He had broken his promise to her.

The sound of the traffic grew louder and he watched the line of cars crawl up the road, led by a high-top truck with Pennine

Hauliers on the box above the cab.

He didn't do anything when the truck passed. A coach came up the hill and he looked through the windscreen to the round face of the man behind the steering wheel. There was bunting strung up over the window.

He imagined a coachload of pensioners on a day trip to the coast, the sort of outing he and Bess swore they would avoid. The passengers would be singing music hall songs and the air inside the coach would be heavy with the scent of Germolene and Parma Violets.

Michael waited until the coach was nearly level with the chair, until he could reach out and touch it, before he stepped out into the carriageway to find Bess.

The Ironmaster's House
Liz Kershaw

The van rattles off down the lane and I am alone in the Ironmaster's garden. The move has taken all day; loading up in Shepherd's Bush, travelling west into Shropshire. It's the middle of September and the summer is turning, folding into brittle leaves and the first hints of wood smoke. The garden is long, a steep bank of straggly grass sweeping from the high, perched house down to the Severn. Dusk comes early in the gorge but the sun still lingers on my part of the river and I go down, careful on the uneven steps, and sit on one of the boulders that jut out from the bank. The water is low, rain-parched, and I watch the weed below the surface move with the flow. The river shimmers with the last of the sunlight. I close my eyes, feel the air cooling as the shadows grow. Listen to the tumbling of shallow rapids.

"This house is just perfect," I tell my father, later, on the phone, "All on its own at the end of an old wagon track. It sort of nestles into the hillside. You'll have to come."

He says he will, when I've settled in. I know he's concerned about disturbing my work.

I reassure him with a lie. "I'm writing already. Don't worry, it'll come back here. I can concentrate. Block all the other stuff out."

He's pleased. Renting the Ironmaster's House was his idea. Then, I hear worry again. "Chrissie, it's not too isolated, is it? You won't start… dwelling on things again?"

"It's fine," I say, and mean it. "It feels a whole lot safer than Shepherd's Bush." I wander to the window, the mobile signal's stronger there. Night has fallen but I can still see flashes of silver as the moon reflects off the river. "And it's only a mile from Ironbridge, a couple of minutes in the car. It's heaving with people there. If I feel lonely, I promise I'll go off and set up in a café to write. Promise."

"You'll be careful though, won't you? Lock up properly? If people get to hear that you're there on your own…"

"Of course. Stop fretting. I'll get the ancestors to look after me. Bet the old Ironmaster won't stand for any nonsense."

I expect a laugh, but there's no reply. Just a crackle, then silence. The line's failed. I mouth, "Night Dad, love you," into the void and turn back to my mound of unpacked boxes.

Before bed, I fetch my torch and go back down to the riverbank. The gorge is famous for flooding but my forebears knew what they were doing when they built this house. It's on high ground, solid ground too, above the landslips, with its sloping garden as a buffer. I look back at it, staunch above me, dark brick, friendly light shining from the windows and I realise that I'm at peace for the first time in months. I'm not worried by its isolation; it already feels familiar, homely, secure. I wish I'd spent the summer here, watching out for swifts and kingfishers, feeling the river breeze in my hair.

I point my torch at the water; the rapids are just downstream, near enough to stir up the quiet of the night. There's a separate sound above the slap and thrust of the flow; a sibilant, long and drawn out 's', repeated over and over. I have a fancy that the river is whispering a welcome to me, calling my name. I hold my breath, trying to listen, and then inhale deeply in reflex. There's a sudden odd tang in the air, acidic, a hint of sulphur. It catches in the back of my throat and I cough. It's fascinating, I think, how a steep gorge will funnel air, or noise, will have its own peculiar rules and environment, be its own world.

As I turn back towards the house, I hear the sound more distinctly, 'sssssss... ssssss.' I swing round, invade the shadows with my torch beam, but there's nothing to see. Nothing to hear, either, as I climb back to the house and the final hiss lisps away into the night.

I sleep well, waking late. The house is shady inside, the bright morning sunlight filtered by the tangled woodland banking up behind the track. I make a quick breakfast and then go out exploring, climbing up through the trees to the topmost part of the gorge.

The path winds between thin, tall trees canopied together, more gold than green now, as the autumn advances. The thorny undergrowth beneath is uneven on the ground, lumpy, like a cloth laid over a table of objects. I part the ivy suckered to the surface of one of the larger piles to find colour beneath: aubergine bricks tumbled into broken heaps; lumps of rough-hewn sandstone; the odd fragment of metal. I realise suddenly that the house would not always have been on its own. The track would have served other houses, cottages; a whole community. My house is a remnant, a solitary descendent, like me.

At the top, the path widens to join fields which splay out across the land. I find a road, strike back down towards the town and buy myself a ticket to all the scattered museums celebrating the cauldron of industry that used to line this ribbon of river valley. Tiles, iron, pottery. White heat bending elements to serve man's purposes. The whole place was forged from fire, I think, fire and metal and the sweat of working men. Now, the old iron bridge dominates it all, links the site of foundries with clay pits, smelting furnaces with sunken iron tracks.

I ask the museum guide, "Was there a village behind the old Ironmaster's House? The one at the end of the track by the river?"

He tells me how the cottages would have clustered around the foundry. How my house would have been deliberately placed some distance apart to protect the Ironmaster's family from the worst of the pollution and disease.

I tell him in return that it was my family, my direct ancestors, who had built the house in the late eighteenth century. "My father's researched the genealogy, but I'd like to find out more about us, how we lived, what sort of people we were." I have imagined men of energy, piety, ingenuity. I add, "When my father was researching, he found that the Ironmaster's house was up for rent, so that's why I'm here. Back to where we started. I'm the last of the line, it seemed right to close the circle."

The guide suggests some useful books, gives me the museum archivist's details. Smiles and says, "Welcome home!"

Back at the house, I phone the archivist, ask if he has any documents specific to my Ironmaster ancestor and his company. He is helpful, but reserved. I press him, and he promises to copy what he can for me. He is busy, he says. Hasn't really got the time to talk at the moment, but the documents should tell me all I need to know.

I settle at my desk, position my notepad and pen and try to breathe away the panic. I'm a successful writer. I have seven novels to my name. I can do this. I can do it again. I stare down. The last words I wrote, several weeks ago in London, written as my life disintegrated around me, intimidate me from the top of the pad.

…Lottie stood by the silver BMW watching Darryl saunter across the car park. Someone nearby had lit a cigarette and the trailing smoke caused a lurch of nausea …

I swallow, inhale again, but as I pick up my pen to continue, I smell burning. I scrape back my chair and leave the sitting room to search for the source. Procrastination, but I should be sensible even though I haven't used the oven or lit a fire yet and the central heating is off. I poke about in all the ground floor rooms, but there's nothing untoward. Back in the sitting room, I smell it again; there's no mistaking it there. Acrid, that hint of sulphur. My shoulders relax. I remember the open window above my desk. The smoke must be coming from outside, the draught must have pulled it through the house. Season of bonfires, I remind myself.

I go outside. The woodland and the track are tranquil and silent; there's no smoke, no sign of a fire. I skirt the house, walk a few yards along the track, double back and descend the full length of the garden. The air is clear and fresh as it skips off the river; the only heat comes from the slant of the afternoon sun.

Back inside, the taint of burning seems to have grown stronger, settled into the furnishings and insinuated itself throughout the ground floor. I resist the desire to go on another search and settle down. It was a freak of the gorge, I think. The way air flows in, catches on the surface of the water and rides with the flow, trapped between the towers of sandstone cliff. Could have been a fire several miles off. Could be a barbecue at the pub downstream. Could be anything, but there's nothing amiss here.

I pick up my pen and suddenly, the words start flowing. The block of grief and mental torment has gone; I am a novelist again. Pictures form in my mind, characters speak to me, Lottie my protagonist is once again real, believable. Alive. My hand moves across the page, the paper smooth under my skin.

… As Lottie turned her head away from the smoke, she heard a voice behind her. "Please …'

I stop. Put a thick line through the sentence. It makes absolutely no sense in the context of this point in the story. I start again, and the sentence reappears. I frown, strike it out. Move Lottie to another location and decide to fill the gap later. Beside her, wherever I place her and always round about the level of her elbow, comes the small, pleading voice. "Please."

I place the pen up on the shelf, away from my desk, look at the page. Line after line of crossed out words in a handwriting that has become erratically spiky.

I wonder whether I should stop resisting and just go with what the voices in my head are telling me. The technique's always worked in the past; what if the move, the change in my circumstances, have altered the story I set out to tell?

I give up on work and go to take a shower. The fabric of my clothes seems to have absorbed the smell of smoke and every movement brings my attention back to it. I wash my hair, scrub my body in bergamot scented foam. Afterwards, I phone my father.

"It's great here," I say, "fabulous. Just what I needed." I pause. "When can you come?"

He suggests a date a month away. I agree. He asks, "And you're okay?"

"Perfectly fine. Really. Relax."

"No more... episodes?"

"No. All that's finished with."

"Writing?"

I fudge a reply.

Late that evening, after night has fallen, I take another walk down the garden. The air tastes damp and peaty; rain soon, I think. The river is churning over the rapids, faster than yesterday. I suspect it has already rained in the borderlands to the north where the river gathers strength. It'll be higher here tomorrow. I'm excited by the prospect of being close to the rhythm of the seasons, watching the Severn changing every day, the leaves turning gold, falling, dying. The frost sparkling on the garden.

Above the rush and swirl of the eddies, I hear the noise again. The long, drawn out 'sssss'. Tonight it is louder, longer. If I didn't know better, that it was a phenomenon of the river's passage, I could imagine it as a voice, and although I know this is nonsense, I stay rigidly still and strain to hear what it is saying. There is an urgency to it, increasing, moving closer and then... I get it, hear its message. "Please. Please. Pleassssssse."

I sleep fitfully and wake at dawn amid whirling images of flames and smoke. In my dream, the river is on fire, a flow of thin red lava with a broken crust of black. I worry at first that the source of yesterday's smoke, whatever it was, has grown stronger, smouldered in the night and infiltrated my unconscious mind, but although the smell of burning is there still, stronger than before, there's nothing visible. There are only the ordinary things. Shady light comes in through the tall kitchen window, washed cups and plates shine on the drainer, a checked tea-towel hangs by the sink.

I enter the sitting room ready for work and my nostrils contract. My eyes smart. I open the window, take my desk chair outside and beat the foam seat to loosen any hint of smoke lodged in the fibres. I think: it's like an exorcism, then tick myself off for being fanciful.

Afterwards, I pick up my pen and a character enters my head. This isn't unusual, most of my characters have walked into my consciousness and onto the page. I try to plan, but I'm a winger, really, a seat of the pants writer. Most times it works.

...Lottie sipped her cappuccino and started at a small movement beside her. A slight young girl, six or seven, had settled at the table next to hers. She was wearing a ragged dress under a sooty pinafore and her hair hung loose down her back. As Lottie looked over at her, the girl turned her head, slowly. One side of her blackened face still showed the delicate beauty of her childhood. The other had been

charred into scorched weeping flesh …

When I scrub out the lines and re-write Lottie into a hotel lift, the girl is there too, reflected back by the mirrored surface of the interior. When Lottie turns and screams, I slam the notebook shut and find that I am shaking.

I run upstairs to the bedroom where the signal is strongest and phone the landlord. I make my tone light and unconcerned. "I'm getting on fine here. I love the Ironmaster's House."

He sounds distant; I've interrupted something. "Fantastic. Glad you like it."

"Just out of interest, did you ever smell burning? I'm worried that the wiring may need checking."

He hasn't, and the house was re-wired fairly recently, but he's happy to ask the electrician to call by.

"Yes, thanks," I say, "better safe than sorry." I pause. "By the way, you didn't hear anything strange either, did you? Down by the river?"

He tells me how much he loved living in the house, only moved because of his job. I'm grateful, reassured. The house is harmless. My mental fragility, my creative imagination, unused to isolation, is not. I give myself a shake, tell myself to get a grip.

That evening, I avoid writing and spend time reading the books I'd bought at the museum shop. The night is cloudless and chill. I coax the open fire into life, find my box of scented candles and arrange them round the room. Lavender. Geranium. I'm hoping that they'll mask the smell of burning which seems to have become mobile, moving with me wherever I go in the house. The corners of any room I'm in become indistinct, hazy, so that the features of walls or furniture are softened, filtered, as if by a fine layer of smoke. If I move over to investigate, the haze disperses, leaving me staring at a perfectly clear part of the room while another clouds up behind me.

I begin to diagnose myself. I'm still not completely well. My imagination is running wild. I'm on my own too much and it's not good for me, whatever I told my father. Maybe the bustle of London had its uses. Tomorrow I'll go into town, pick up the documents from the archivist and have lunch at one of the inns on the Wharfage. I'll find strangers to talk to, lift myself out of these fantasies.

I open a window at the front, try to loosen the wheezing in my chest. I stare out beyond the track at the woodland, think of the remains of the foundry and cottages beneath it. The trees are silhouetted black against the ink blue of the windless night, perfectly still. Gradually, I become aware that there is a new sound in the air. A hum, liked the merged voices of a crowd, individuality and words lost in the mass. I'm unnerved until I remember again how the valley plays tricks with acoustics as well as air currents, sounds bouncing off the sheer walls of the gorge to rebound a mile downriver. It will be the revellers along the riverside, the pubs spilling out onto the pavement.

I return to my reading. The new books are starting to paint a picture of the area in its industrial glory days. The night sky flashing scarlet and gold, lit up by furnaces sparking like a run of miniature volcanos. The noise never abating, clashing, roaring, the clanking of wheels, working animals beaten and complaining, men shouting, babies crying uncomforted. The houses jammed together, open drains behind, disease seeping out to take the lives of the weak and unlucky. I read on. Flames rise in the grate as the kindling catches and fuels the coal. The candles flicker. The smell of burning overpowers the gentle flower oils, advancing from each corner, catching at my throat and although I am certain that my mind is the magician of all this, I throw down the book, pull my torch off the shelf and leave the house, taking the path down the garden at a half run.

The night is still, the river has calmed and there is less extraneous noise to cover the pleading voice. It's louder, more defined, insistent. "Please. Please. Please." A clear, high voice: a woman's? Or perhaps a child's? Above me, in the woodland, the rumble of the crowd is strengthening too. I imagine a mob, the tone urgent and angry, advancing down the hill towards the track and I look up, but I see no movement, no sign of any life.

I run back inside and lock the doors. The fire in the sitting room has settled down a fraction, the candles are stronger, the wax melting and sending its perfume to mask the smell of burning. It's cosy, now, and the imaginings I had outside seem stupid; hysterical. I'd had the feeling, staring up at the woods beyond the house, of being swamped by the misery of the people who had built this area's prosperity; a collective wretchedness which had soaked down into the land like fetid water, stayed trapped, fermenting in the sandstone, now rising, flowing. Pressing down towards me.

The homeliness of the room shames me. How can I have been so irrational to think that I was some sort of catalyst for the release of ancient despair?

I pick up the phone, go upstairs, find the number. When he answers, I swallow, try to ignore the carbon taste in my mouth. "Hi, Dad."

"Hello? Chrissie?" I sense that he is checking the time. Too late for regular calls. He asks if I'm okay.

"Yes, fine. No problems," I reply, too quickly. "I'm sorry if I startled you, didn't realise how late it was. I'm keeping odd hours, you know how it is when I'm writing. Just fancied a chat." I imagine him, cardigan and reading glasses on, and I feel security creep down through me like a warm milky drink.

There's a pause, "Sorry, sweetheart, but I can't chat right now."

"No?" I feel like he's slapped me.

He lowers his voice, tells me he has a friend, Valerie, around for a meal and drinks.

68

A friend. Valerie. Still there so late. I ring off, close the windows to shut out the echoing voices. Bury my face in my pillow. Where have you gone, Dad? Why does everyone always leave me? I make my trip into town the next day to collect the archivist's information, enjoy a salad at a sunny courtyard table and watch the tourists snap the symmetrical curves of the famous bridge. Once again, my imaginings ebb away in the ordinariness of the scene, and I make a resolution. By the end of the afternoon, I've achieved it; gained a two-afternoon a week job in the museum tea-shop. What I lose in writing time I will gain in stimulation, I think. And why not go with the strange little child character who has appeared in my writing? Change direction. Write something historical. I'm in the right place for inspiration, after all.

That evening, I pick up my notebook, trying not to look at the haze blurring the corner of the room. There is a grainy deposit, like coal dust, over all the surfaces and the smell of smoke has deepened and concentrated. Each breath stings the back of my throat, catches in my chest. It'll be the fire disturbing the soot in the unswept chimney, or a down-draft forcing the smoke the wrong way. Something logical, of this world. I know I need to confront and conquer this idiocy, bring it out into the open. I have let the flat in Shepherd's Bush, made a year commitment to the Ironmaster's house. I will not become how my mother was, filtering life through a set of net curtains.

I stand up, speak out, "None of this is real. I have become a victim of my own mind."

There is a rustle, the fire sparks. The haze in the corner thickens and shifts towards me. I try to speak again, but I know my voice has lost its confidence, is weak, mollifying. "What can I do? I ask. "How can I help you, whoever or whatever you are?"

The candles flicker then burn again, more brightly. I hear the high clarity of a child's voice, just outside the window by one of the lower panes. "Please."

"I will help you," I say, "if you let me know what I can do. I can't help if I don't know who you are or what you want from me."

There is no reply, but I catch a different noise: the roar of the mob has returned outside the house. It – they – must have crossed the track, must be close to the front door. Child at the back, mob at the front … I rush upstairs to see but there is nothing. No one there. Not even a leaf moves.

Back at the bottom of the stairs, I slide and nearly fall, saving myself by grabbing at the banister. A fine layer of ash, bone-grey and gritty, has made the tiles slippery. As I correct my balance, I see that the ash has been disturbed by a set of child-sized footprints leading back into the sitting room.

"Please!" I say it now, my plea, directed everywhere. I can feel sweat prickling under my arms, my heart racing. "Please let me know what I can do to help you?"

There is no answer. Above the crowd outside, I hear individual shouts, a woman crying, and I cover my ears, following the footprints into the room and over to the desk. The documents the archivist had copied for me lie scattered all over it; I had left them neatly stacked and I know, I am sure, that I have not disturbed them. Now, they are a jumbled mess: snatches of the history of the house and the ironmasters and overseers who had lived there; reports on the conditions of the tenants on the hill, a list of births and deaths. I remember the archivist's tone when I'd told him my name, so proud of my local credentials. "Chrissie Bowen. I'm descended from Samuel Bowen, the Ironmaster." The withdrawal in it, the reserve.

I need to know, now. I need to know what happened. I sit down, pick up my pen. Start a new page of the notebook. My hand, as before, moves without any conscious thought.

I write a description of the Ironmaster's House as it was when first built; panelled walls, solid oak furniture, wooden floor in the parlour covered with a woollen rug, candles mellow in glass shades, bible on the sideboard; everything plain but good quality.

I describe a man, well-built, in his late forties, short cropped hair, flecked with grey. He is dozing, his feet propped on a footstool, a leather-bound ledger lying across his worsted trousers. He has removed his wig and set it at his side.

... There is a knock at the front door, urgent and demanding. The man barely registers it but someone else takes notice and soon, the door to the parlour opens and a maid enters. She clears her throat, tugging nervously at her apron. "I'm sorry, sir, but there's a lady at the door. From the cottages."

He opens one eye. "Tell her to go away, girl. It's late. She can see me in the office tomorrow."

"But sir, she's got a child with her."

"Do I need to repeat myself?"

"No, sir."

The maid disappears but soon returns. This time, the man in the chair pulls himself up into a more upright position. His complexion is reddening. "What now, girl?"

"Please Mr Bowen, sir, she won't go away. She's sat on the step."

The man mutters and stands up. He pushes past the maid and goes to the front door, his nailed boots ringing on the tiles. He flings open the door, but says nothing. His face is set in lines of fury.

A woman sits on the stone step. She is holding a child, a slight girl of around six or seven. The girl is wrapped in a filthy blanket, her feet bare. She is silent and seems to be drifting in and out of consciousness. The woman is pinched with fear and fatigue, runnels of tears carve through the dirt on her face. She struggles to her feet, dragging the child up with her, and says, "Please sir, she's been burnt at the furnace. She needs help."

"Madam," the man says, "I am not the Doctor."

"We haven't got no money for the Doctor, sir."

He shrugs, starts to turn away, says, "In that case, you will not be seen by him. I am confounded as to the reason for your appearance at my door."

The woman says, "Please sir, will you give us some money for the Doctor? She was hurt doing your work, in your foundry."

The man stares. His face colours scarlet, his pale eyes protrude. Behind him the maid backs down the hallway. He says, "How dare you disturb me like this! How dare you come to my house begging, begging for money, madam, because you have been too profligate to lay sufficient aside for your family!"

The woman stands her ground, looks at him directly. The child is almost too heavy for her to hold and the strain makes her voice rise. "You've always said you're a man of God, sir. Will you help a child now? Please?"

The child opens her eyes, her mouth forms a word but the sound is faint, like a ripple in the breeze over the river. "Please."

The man seems not to hear the child and steps forward, striking the woman so hard on the shoulder that she staggers backwards and nearly drops the child. The man spits anger at her. "How dare you talk back to me like that! Go! And take that disgusting bundle of rags with you." He wheels round and slams the door, screams, "Girl!"

I drop the pen with a yelp of pain. It has burned my fingers. The room is searing, furnace hot. The fire blazes in the hearth, the candle pillars are collapsing into liquid. In the corner, another set of flames are flickering, licking around the skirting board, fanning up towards the curtains. Outside, the shouting and crying is growing louder, the walls seem to be shivering with the force.

I shout, "It wasn't me! I would have given you the money! Let me be! Please!"

The curtains catch alight, sparks fly onto the desk and the

archivist's documents start to smoulder. I spring up, bat at the flames with my notebook, flick the papers away. The flames by the far wall are ceiling high. I can see the small, still form of a child standing within them. Her arms are outstretched, one side of her face is melting.

I run to the door, force it open, stumble down the garden to the river. The cottagers' voices are all around, screaming, vengeful, jeering, triumphant. My lungs are choked with smoke, pain shoots through the exposed nerve endings of my burnt hands. The Severn is swollen, black in the darkness, flowing steadily down through the history of the gorge, sliding over a river bed scarred with shards of pottery, tiles, rusting parts of machines. Behind me, I can hear the house burning, windows bursting open with the heat. I feel the force of the crowd, pushing me onwards, urging me. There is only one direction I can go.

The water shocks me with its cold. My muscles seize tight with cramp. As I try to move, I look back.

The house stands proud on the rise. There is a low light in the parlour window; my desk lamp pooling over my work. The other windows are shadowed and dark. Unbroken. There are no voices apart from my own as I grasp for the bank, fingers scraping for purchase along an overhanging branch, legs tugged by the vicious current of the rapids. My arms strain, weaken. I drag in a breath of the river air; clear and pure, and I cry, ""Please, please can someone help me? Please!"

For Sale
Pascale Presumey

He left marks on our lives.

1. Wendy house, painted blue and pink. Sparkly curtains hung at the window.
2. Barbecue. Made of carved breeze blocks. Strangely reminiscent of Stonehenge.
3. Side gate. Painted cream. Wrought iron handle. Number of the house encrusted within a heart.
4. Leaf blower. In the shed, hidden behind crates. Empty.
5. Strange tool by outdoor tap. Long rusty pole with handle at one end and fork-like prongs at the other. Why?
6. Cupboard. Difficult to open. No handles.
7. Creaking floorboards. 7 nails missing.
8. Black streaks like distressed plane trails along the floor, the tracks of heavy, stomping boots.
9. Small wooden box. Empty now but once contained medicine packets, cigarette papers, phone numbers scribbled on torn scraps, buttons, an enamelled butterfly.
10. Calendar with mysterious dates highlighted: 22nd of April. No explanation. 29th of August. My birthday. "My" underlined.
11. Walking stick. Bamboo. Unscrews. Contains a spike.
12. Car windscreen wiper. Broken.

13. Coffee table. Crack along the length of the box, where the large heavy boots came down most nights: time to relax a little.

14. Black smear on the wall. A door slammed.

15. Door, paint stripped by two kicks. Door hinges unreliable.

16. Shelf above the hearth. Wobbly. Loosened by a fist.

17. Sofa. Stained when blood seeped into the leather. Indelible. Unscrubbable. There, plain to see every time we sit down: time to relax a little.

18. Indentation in the carpet under the bed, where the knife lay for fifteen years.

Feel free to look around. Touch, smell, listen, that's all fine. Character, they call it, history. Smears, scratches, bruises, the old house creaks and moans with them. But these are not the marks that will remain. Cupboards can be fixed, doors repainted. The nicks and cuts and weeping wounds inside may not be so easily handled.

Could I interest you in a drawer full of letters: thick, gorged with invectives, rebuttals, games, pleading, taunting, threatening, begging, mocking? We all love a bit of drama, don't we?

The ashes in the hearth? Remnants of diaries written by a teenager, found and read by a grown man, consumed and spat up to sting, nag, dig. The diaries stopped, years of silence. Now the few words left are a little burnt round the edges, stained, soiled, their meaning turned into something bad, something wrong, something false. Turning me into the person he claimed I was, a person I hope never existed. But it's hard to judge these days.

Help yourself to one photograph at least. Of another woman with children. Does that woman, wherever she is, hold in her hands a photograph of me and my children? Does she look at us, puzzled, sickened by a melange of scorn and nausea? Did he say I love you? Of course he did. Did he swear forever? Why wouldn't he? I did. Did they laugh in the car until they cried and held hands until they hurt? Did they have their favourite restaurant, their favourite lake, their favourite drink? It's guaranteed. Good times! There have to be good times or the story can never start. Did he whisper words in her ear at night? Words like snakes that writhed and swirled inside her head, spreading poison through her like a red river branching out into small streams here, there, everywhere; reaching every cell, every atom, taking ownership of not just her body. A pillow talk of death. Did he place a knee on her belly, a hand around her throat to make her understand? If she didn't tell her children, it is unlikely she would tell me.

Sit, try the ripped armchair, mind the cracked table, yes these are probably coffee stains on the ceiling. Take it all, go on. It's all tat: old, broken and dirty. I don't want anything for it. There was a time I wished for things but nobody visited then. I could have done with a stranger walking round the house, putting his nose into our business but where were you then, where were you? No, don't go. It's not you, you know that. Sit down, I'll make us some tea. You could say the same thing to me. Where was I? Where the fuck was I? I don't know. I was lost, I had no idea where I was. And even now, I couldn't tell you for sure.

Who are you to tell me it will be alright and how could you know? As you sit here with your thick hands and your heavy eyelids, can you say for certain he will never again appear by the back door, bang hard and loud until he is let in and take over the house again? Throwing himself on the sofa, changing the channel, telling us where to sit, what to do, where to go next. And the commands:

Stop thinking.

Stop.

Sit down here with me.

Stay! Like a dog, an obedient dog, loyal, one who will never talk back.

I never saw the dead body in the cheap pine box, you see. I never put a pin in his eyes, a stake in his heart to make sure he could never come back. When I was a kid, we had sticky paper pinned to the ceiling to catch flies, a swirl of sticky paper right above the kitchen table. We'd eat dinner and I'd watch the flies trying to get away from the yellow gloop. I never saw one make it. Maybe if they could have ripped their own wings off, they would have come unstuck but can a fly live without wings? You don't know. Neither do the flies.

I'm sorry. I'm making you uncomfortable. Are you afraid of ghosts? The rattling of his chains or the wailing in the night does not bother me. It's not his roaming through the house I fear the most but the squatting in my head, the kidnapping of my souvenirs, memories vandalised, dreams burnt in the hearth. What if he has taken all I have in there, ravaged the attic, and I am left empty and locked up forever? What then?

Yes, I know, you have to leave. Go then, go, like the others. And shut the door behind you.

The Last Train to Sóller
Fiona Joseph

The engine hisses and whistles, in preparation for its departure.
Just as I'm about to give up, convinced my plan will fail, I spot
her from my carriage window. She's attempting to run along the
platform, hobbled by the close-fitting cut of her dress, and hin-
dered by shoes designed for strolling, not a last-minute dash for a
train in the Mallorcan heat. A fond smile spreads over my lips.

Until I see the man striding alongside her.

My first reaction is to tell myself he's not with her. An answer-
ing voice in my head says, "Yes he is, you fool, that's her bag he's
carrying."

A bell clangs, like a starting pistol. The man throws the bag
onto the train as it begins to move and grabs her hand to pull
them both on board.

I'd prepared myself for this eventuality. This is what you
expected. This doesn't change things. Even so, the sight of him
with her, and the overnight bag, winds me like a punch to the
solar plexus, wiping the smile clean off my face.

He looks composed as they come down the aisle, but she can't
contain her panting giggles of relief. It's unlikely that she'd recognise me, it has been ten years, but because I sense an encounter
would alarm her, I tilt my white fedora so that it covers most of
my face. They stop at the seats across the aisle and she flings her
bag down onto the wooden bench. Barely three metres

separate us.

Her voice is still clear and sonorous. "I thought we were going to miss it. Are we lucky or what?"

Kismet or karma? Destiny or divine providence? Something greater than coincidence has brought me to this seat, on this train, making this particular journey.

We grind through the outskirts of Palma, past industrial estates and scruffy apartment blocks. Cars whizz past us, their drivers keen to escape the day's swelter and return home to kiss their loved ones.

The man unfolds a brochure. I hear the paper crackle as he shakes it out in front of him. "Sixteen miles to Sóller. Journey time one hour." He starts reciting from the guide, telling her how this Mallorcan village became the centre of the orange growing industry in the 1920s; how our train is nicknamed the 'Vitamin C Express' because it was used to transport the orange harvest between Sóller and Palma.

"Do you know these are all the original fittings? This is real mahogany," he says, knocking the panelling beneath his window. She's playing the game, pretending she hasn't heard all this before.

I tip my hat back, risk a peep. The years have been good to her. Her hair is below her shoulders, worn loose now, a shade or two lighter. I don't recall the amber pendant around her neck. The watch is different too, gold, a timeless, grown-up choice. There's an expensive veneer about her now. She's shinier, tougher. I wonder if her skin still smells and tastes the same.

About him there is little to say. He's a serious-looking guy, short-haired, average height, a runner's build, handsome in a conventional way. A more objective observer would say they are a good match, easy on the eye. One could imagine the fit of their bodies, tight like jigsaw pieces.

She spreads out a picnic of figs, tiny pastries and bottled water on a white napkin. "I pinched this lot at lunchtime today. Compensation for that boring-as-hell plenary we had to sit through. Am I wicked?"

"Christ, I hope so." He dips his head and tries to kiss her, but she turns away, smiling to herself. Delaying the moment. He shifts in his seat, discomfited by his arousal.

He hasn't fucked her. Not yet.

Somewhere between Son Reus and Santa Maria I notice they're holding hands, their palms pressed together and held down in the gap between their bodies.

The voice in my head asks me again, what is it you want? I thought I had a plan, I thought it was to find what the analysts call closure, but seeing her up close after all this time my resolve is like sand, slipping through my fingers. She doesn't know I've kept an eye on her all these years. You can track anybody these days if you look hard enough. And if you have all the time in the world, as I do. I'm just not sure if I'm ready for this, ready to let go of hope.

Now I wonder if I've made the worst possible mistake finding her. I'm an insect; she's the amber that traps me.

Every illicit liaison begins with one or both parties asking the question, have you done this before? This time it's him who asks.

"There was someone… once." She speaks as if she's in a confession box, about to declare everything before she gives herself to this man.

I shut my eyes and slide down a little in my seat. Anyone who could see me might mistake me for a contented chap settling down to hear a good story on the radio. But there's an ache in the space where my heart used to be, like the phantom pain felt by people who've lost a limb.

"He was someone I worked with. We were the youngest, most attractive in our department. It was almost like our colleagues

80

expected it of us." She's probably smiling up at him now, judging how far she can go. "You know how these things happen. All it needs is a set of circumstances, the right opportunity to fall from the sky."

She pauses and I lift my hat slightly to see her gazing into the distance, but I doubt she's taking in the mountain views and the hillside villages. Perhaps she's wondering, as I am, how to convey the ferocity and tenderness of our first, our only, night together; of the way she unlocked the hotel room and held the door open until I'd gone inside, then followed me and let it shut softly behind us. Of how we were on each other in an instant, tearing and frantic, before the fire settled to slowly burn all night long.

The guard wanders through our coach and announces a fifteen minute photo stop at Mirador Pujol D'en Banya.

"I need to stretch my legs," he says. "Coming?"

She shakes her head. "You go."

On the platform, he raises his arms above his head and lets them swing down. He takes a mobile from his trouser pocket, holds it up to check the signal, no doubt so he can send the perfunctory text to his wife. Conference a bore, same old faces, shouldn't have come, missing you. The guard comes out for a cigarette. The man says a few words, offers him notes and the guard's expression changes from puzzlement to understanding. He disappears for a few moments, then returns and slaps the man on the back and hands him a packet. Condoms.

Will he make her cry out like I did?

Suddenly it strikes me that I've missed an opportunity. Idiot! I could jump off this train and toss him over the fence like a human caber, and send him tumbling down the slope into the forest where his spine will snap in two as it hits a tree.

But he's strolling back now, ready to climb on board.

She takes out her make up bag, glances at her phone and

then applies lipstick, contorting her mouth while she looks in a compact mirror. She moves the mirror around to check her hair and then snaps it shut. From the corner of my eye I can see the platinum band is still on her left hand. Yup, still married. Still playing away.

I'd forgotten about the tunnels. The first time we plunge in the noise is deafening, and the temperature drops so suddenly it's like being doused with ice-cold water. To begin with it feels pitch-black until we get used to the dim glow of the tungsten ceiling lights, which cast their yellow pallor over the skin. Then, just as quickly, we're out in the warmth and daylight again and passing the olive groves of Bunyola, the low tree branches swishing against our windows.

Go on, tell him, I want to say. I want to hear her get to the part where she told me she wanted to make her marriage work.

"I don't think of him every day. That would be untrue, but I do think of him a lot." I shift slightly so I can see her face. Her eyes are welling up, and he's reaching for her, putting his arm around her shoulders. "Have you ever been out somewhere," she says, "in a shop or a bar and there's music playing? And suddenly you hear a song you've never heard before and it sounds perfect. You listen, entranced, totally caught up in those few minutes, and then it ends, it's over. And all the time you were listening a part of you knew you'd never hear that song again, you'd never be touched in the same way."

He seems moved, his self-interest and ambition for tonight put to one side. "It's not too late, is it?"

"It's been too late for a long time." She fondles the pendant while she speaks. "Just because you choose the right path doesn't mean you never have any regrets, or imagine what might have been. I still picture holding his hand, walking in a market, sitting in a pub, chatting while I cook for him, we're always talking in my day dreams. Mundane stuff." She sighs. "You could say we were lucky. We never got to put it to the test." All the melancholy has restored the original beauty to her face, wiped away the last ten years.

He pulls her close and the first tears spill. "He would have been thirty-five today," she says. It's hard to look at her face crumpling, so instead I watch him while he takes in the information, pieces together the last bit of the story.

And then we enter the final tunnel before Sóller.

Only this time there's no chill, no roaring, and no shadowy light. Just a calm that spreads through me like a tranquiliser, erasing all my thoughts, and pain. No more struggle. We're close to our destination now. The descent into the town of Sóller is so steep it can make the ears pop. Our train is flanked either side by the famous orange plantations. The trees are so close you can reach out and pick their fruit, yours for the taking.

She's tracing a pattern on his chest with her fingertip. "About tonight," she says. "Might be best if we have separate rooms. Sorry if I've led you on, been a tease, it's just that it doesn't feel..."

Sometimes all you need is to hear the words.

I look down to the dusty floor of our carriage as the train begins to slow, and then I rest my head against the window.

Sóller looks as beautiful as ever. Brilliant white and sugar-pink houses shimmer in the dying sun, plane trees hazy in the distance. The scent of the sea mingles with the citrus perfume of oranges.

With a balled-up tissue she pats underneath her eyes. He holds her cardigan behind her while she tries to find the armholes, and misses. It makes them laugh. He swings her bag over his shoulder and they get off the train. I hope they'll catch a tram to the port, and that she'll take him to a seaside cafe, where they'll drink the freshly-pressed juice from the orange groves, and kiss and whisper and hold hands all the way to their hotel.

Edith
Ray Robinson

Black desolate hills, imposing but bleakly beautiful. Jake stands on the sopping fell listening to the hish of the nearby pine trees shifting on the pith of the wind. Ahead of him, on the horizon, an isolated building. The Ox pub.

He blows onto his fingertips, cold roses of burn. He pinches the bridge of his nose between finger and thumb and discharges an oyster of snot. Inhales: the astringent smell of the pines. A strand of hair falls in front of his face and he licks his palm and slicks the hair across his pate.

"Come on."

He turns up his collar and heads towards the Ox.

He sits in his usual chair in the old smoking snug, a wooden curved affair decorated with old lamps and framed black and whites of the valley two fathers ago. The nearest picture shows people ice-skating on the river back when winters got cold enough. He likes to imagine he is one of the children in the image, skating arabesques.

The pub is quiet. The barmaid checks up on him now and then, flimflamming about nothing in particular as she leans over the bar proffering an eyeful of cleavage.

"Same again, Jake?"

"Aye. Cheers."

He glances down at the local newspaper. The article on the front page is about a thirteen-year-old girl gone missing from a neighbouring town. He squints at the girl's open face and then folds the paper and places it on the stool next to him. The barmaid brings his ale through and removes his empty glass and leaves. Jake stares down at the dark liquid for a long time, and then checks the clock on the wall. Before long, Sheila pops her head around the door.

"You all right for a drink there, Jake?"

He nods, beams.

Sheila is well known around town. Bottle blonde hair and rotisserie tan. Geordie, fleshy. Mouth on her. String of errant kids all grown up and gone. Jake likes her crass laughing talk. Sees something noble in her. Honest.

Two minutes later, she parks her ample arse beside him and sips at her house double vodka and coke. As per, she starts rattling on about her mother, giving Jake the same dispassionate rundown. Jake has known Sheila's mother for 60-odd years, a spirited sparrow with a shock of dyed red hair. Once a looker, she was now the old bat who slept in her living room chair at night with the curtains open for all and sundry.

A song starts playing on the jukebox. Sugar Baby Love. Sheila begins to sway, humming, jostling him.

"Howay," she says. "Let's have a boogie."

She gets to her feet and extends a hand.

"Don't talk daft."

She steps away, moves her hips and shakes her hair. Under the ceiling light, she looks pretty. Jake lets his eyes wander her body and something in his stomach churns.

The barmaid appears at the hatch, a smirk on her face.

"Same again youse two?"

Jake nods and averts his gaze, focussed on the pictures on the walls until the song comes to an end and Sheila collects the drinks from the hatch and plonks herself next to Jake, breathless.

Jake chortles.

Sheila asks, "What?"

The noise coming from the bar area is slightly louder now. Leaning forward, Sheila lays a small, chubby hand on Jake's. Moist. Hot.

"You never say much, do you, hon?"

He stares at her hand.

"I like that in a man."

"Edith," he says. "Used to vex her, like."

Uttering her name discharges a pulse of regret. He looks pained. He feels it first in his stomach and then it spreads to his limbs. He pulls his hand away and sits it in his lap.

Later. Clamour from the bar and the lamps flickering into life as Sheila enters with the fifth round. She places the whiskey chaser next to his ale.

Jake tuts. "I shouldn't."

"Because whiskey makes you frisky?"

"They're on my tab right?"

"Oh shush."

"I'm not letting no woman pay for my drink."

"Dinosaur."

Ignoring her, he lifts the glass to his nose and sniffs the peat. She clinks his glass, almost hitting him in the face.

"Up your bum," she says.

"It's to be savoured."

"Ahw get it down your neck, man."

"Guess it might help wash it down."

"Wash what down?"

Jake slugs the whiskey and wipes his mouth.

"Nowt."

Then he sees her. Edith. She's standing beside the door, arms folded, a disapproving look on her face. It's like she's really there, so real it's disturbing. But he blinks and she's gone.

He searches Sheila's face for some sort of reaction. Her mouth is moving and Jake tunes in for a second.

"I always thought they were a bit, you know, shifty-looking..."

This is the first time he's seen Edith in public, not just at home in his private moments. Drunk, fearful of seeing her again, it feels like everything is slipping away from him. He looks older, weak, vulnerable. He scans the room nervously, suspiciously. Keeps expecting her to reappear.

Sheila witters on in full-throated ease.

The burning returns, a scorching to his lower abdomen and a sudden flush of panic loosens things even more. He leans over, clutching his stomach.

"Just spend a penny."

He stands unsteadily, holding onto the table, then heads for the door.

"That's the problem with beer," Sheila shouts behind him. "You only get to rent it."

Regulars acknowledge him as he lumbers by. The Gents is empty. Leaning against the wall above a urinal, struggling with the front of his trousers, he realises he needs to shit and staggers towards the cubicle and stops, twining his legs, but they buckle and with a look of surprise he stumbles and lands with a jolt on his knees, slumping onto his side. A ragged exhale.

Lying there for what seems like the longest time, shaking now. The vegetal stench. Shock of pain. He is trying to move each of his limbs in turn when something drifts down from the ceiling, a skelter of leaves falling from the branches of a tree. He feels them landing on his hand, his face.

It's happening again.

He's in the backwoods, entering that dire memory, fearful not of its respite but of waking up beside Edith's body again and realising that the memory is where he longs to be. To tell himself that the smell is not her smell, not the smell of death, sniffing his fingers for a trace of jojoba. And as the leaves clear he sees a young man walking briskly through the trees…

Jake was twenty-two and crouching behind a bush, watching the man, handsome, greased-up quiff, enter the derelict cottage. Edith was waiting inside, dressed for a night out, bouffant hair and pastel blue suit. Jake had followed her here, his suspicions getting the better of him, proving him right.

Picturing Edith inside, her skirt pulled up among the mess, he buried his face in his hands and heaved.

The ding of the microwave brings him back into the present. He is in his dressing gown, hair damp, slicked back, sitting in the chair next to the gas fire, a greasy stain on the antimacassar behind him. The farmhouse-style kitchen is a state of dust and chaos and half-eaten meals. The washing machine whirs into another cycle, banging in the utility room. Sheila takes the mug of soup from the microwave and passes it to him.

"Here."

He peers up at her.

"You've done enough now, lass. I'll be right."

She places her hands on her hips, breathing a sigh down at him. The smell of alcohol on her breath makes him avert his face. He rubs his left leg, left arm. He'll feel it tomorrow. Sheila places a hand on his shoulder and squeezes but it does nothing to assuage his shame.

"Jake, man."

"Said I'm fine."

"I made a start on the dishes, but flaming hell. You need someone in here, pet."

He stares down into his cup of soup.

She asks, "How long's it been?"

"What?"

"Since Edith passed?"

Pause. "Four."

"Four month and you're not coping, are you."

It isn't a question.

He turns to look at a framed photograph on the mantelpiece. He squints at it, as if struggling to jettison some distasteful memory. The picture is old, the Kodachrome hues of an early Polaroid: their son, William, standing beside the beck cradling a mid-size rainbow trout in both hands, beaming into the camera.

Sheila asks, "Who's that?"

"Our lad."

Jake looks at her. She looks at him.

"Your grandson?'

"No."

Pause. "Where is he?"

Jake's stare turns inward.

"I'm not…"

He indicates the photo again, raising a shaking finger, but he can't speak for crying which comes upon him suddenly.

"Ahw, Jake man."

"I'm…"

His voice fails. He tries again.

"… a coward."

He's crying now and telling himself, "Don't. Not here."

You can tell she wants to hug him but she's shocked to see him like this.

Misinterpreting him, she says, "Shush. I told you not to fret. We all need to cut loose now and then. Besides, it's my fault for getting you so drunk. As long as you're OK?"

They both have tears in their eyes as Jake drops his mug of

soup on the floor and shouts, "Go away!"

He's on his feet. Sheila recoils. Behind her, Edith stands, a young woman again – that lovely slip of a thing he met at the factory gates – laughing soundlessly.

He could reach over, touch her.

But then, presently, she's gone.

He searches the room. Sheila glances around.

"What is it?"

He knows exactly what Edith was laughing about. The anger rises in him, palpable.

"I said out!"

"Don't throw a wobbler with me, you old bugger."

Rooted to the spot, he points towards the door.

"Get!"

"Jake..."

"I said out of my bastard house!"

Sat in bed among dim lamplight and stale shadows, mould climbing the walls between curls of wallpaper. It's cold in the room but his pyjama top is unbuttoned, exposing a scribble of white chest hair. Hail plinks the guttering and windowsill outside, a few pellets making it through the part-opened window, flicking the curtain so. Nights like these, when a load of weather moseys around the hills and leaves a stillness and smell of earth behind, he likes that better than anything.

He runs his fingers over the dress spread out next to him, sliding his nails into the crimped folds at the waist.

"Come on," he says. "Rise and shine."

He glances towards the window. Through cobwebs and husks of dead flies, the starless sky hangs framed like a blackboard, within it, the cold yellow light of the farmhouse on the opposite hillside. Distantly, a dog barks. Then a second dog starts. Canine serenade.

The farmer must be getting the cows ready for milking, collies nipping their ankles. Sometimes Jake stands by the window in the pre-dawn, waiting for the farmer's bedroom light to come on, a kind of company.

He pats the dress, sniffs his fingers. Nothing.

He eyes the bedside table: a large-print Western novel, a glass of water containing his dentures, a jar of women's hand lotion, and a framed black and white photograph. He stares at the image...

It was 1968. They were standing on a beach together with the sea in the background, the resort off-season empty, everything burnished to grey-scale apart from Edith in her pastel blue suit. Jake sported his Sunday best, booted and suited, country provincial.

Edith said, "Thought you'd be pleased."

And he said, "Course. I am."

"We've been trying so long, Jake. I'd..."

How he shook her arm from his and turned to face the sea. Glanced at her sideways and then back. She was crying now. He stared at the waves for the longest time, feeling so wrong, and then he softened.

"Come here," he said, enveloping her in his arms, and after a long moment, he said, "you're going to be a great mum..."

Jake sighs, his breath fogging the bedroom air. He wipes the icy slub of his nose and inhales. Yes. Smell of jojoba.

Later. Dawn creeps through the window mixing with the low-watt glow of the bedside lamp. His joints ache from lying still for so long. Outside the window, a blackbird begins going through his songbook for the day, followed by a noise beyond the bedroom door. There she is, walking the landing with heavy-heeled steps, making her way downstairs. The creak of the second riser.

He reaches over and takes the jar of jojoba hand lotion from his bedside table and sits it in his lap for a moment before unscrewing the lid.

There: the ghostly contours of Edith's fingerprints, frozen in time.

Tall, skinny, sallow, he wears a tired-looking suit and four-day salt and pepper beard, his iron-grey hair slicked back. He may once have been handsome but now looks haunted by time.

He pauses to listen behind the kitchen door, as, faintly, she hums along to the radio.

Then her voice from behind the door: "Brew?"

Jake smiles. "Cheers love."

He heads into the living room where bright morning light falls aslant through a gap in the tired curtains, illuminating a mishmash of ugly large wooden furniture and psychedelic carpets, his shirt and underpants hanging to dry on the horse beside the hearth.

He sits on the settee, picks up his brogues and dribbles a glob of spit down onto the toe, rubbing it in with his sleeve. He considers turning the gas fire on but she'll only moan. He misses building a real fire, listening to the house click and sigh.

He stares at the blank cataract of the TV screen wishing he knew what to do.

She enters, nothing but a motion blur. In her wake, motes of dust curl through a beam of sunlight. She often wafts into the room smelling of perfume and hairspray, and here, now, he inhales the air as she passes him a mug of hot sweet tea, handle first, and then groans as she takes her place beside him.

Sips. Sighs.

"Grand that," she says.

He blinks at the blank TV screen where the room's cambered,

monochrome reflection reveals the truth: an old man sitting alone on a settee holding an imaginary mug of tea.

They are silent.

Eventually she asks, "Are you all right?"

"No, I'm half left."

"You want the telly on?"

Jake continues to stare at the TV.

She says, "I said, you want the telly on?"

"Deaf now am I, as well as daft?"

She mutters something under her breath. The light in the room dims. Jake pauses, listens, searching the room.

"Edith?"

He reaches out with both hands, palms flat, pushing outwards into the dimness of the room. Feels the walls of his loneliness getting stronger.

The night time storm has wiped the sky to a baby blue. Poised between the cemetery gates, a bouquet of daisies in each hand, he peers up at the church clock as it nears noon.

He recalls the morning exactly twelve months back, sitting on the edge of the bed with Edith's arms around his shoulders, helping her on with her tights. How they made their way out into the morning, heading across the moor and down into town, the High Street busy with the usual workday sight.

How they went to the florists to buy the same bouquet they did every year, eighteen daisies for each year they were blessed with him, and how the florist always looked at Jake with something like pity and Jake wanted to punch the man.

How, at the graveside, they would lay the flowers against the headstone and Edith would talk to their boy like he was down in the ground listening.

How Jake would recall the first time he held William's tiny body in his arms. William's new and startled, big blue eyes.

And how Jake stood at the graveside like that, holding Edith's hand, unable to reach her through all these years.

The church bell begins to toll. Then, trying to work out why he's come here, he starts back the way he came.

At the edge of the park he exits the kissing gate and begins the climb up the steep cobbles and then along the winding dirt track, still carrying the bouquets either side of him. He stops a few times to catch his breath, peering out across the hills, at the village below: the witch's hat of the church spire, the corrugated roof of the paper mill, diseased windpipe of the canal.

It begins to drizzle and blow, sheep making their plaintive noises in the field beside him. He moves on.

Distantly, the ramshackle cottage. Four sagging right angles of mossy tumbling stone. Render fallen from the walls. Small trees growing from the wrecked roof and gabling. Nature assimilating his memories, regrets. He observes the place, thinking.

Standing on the threshold peering in. Remnants of dirty curtains at the windows, a few of the panes still intact. On the floor, in front of the fireplace, the bones of some long-dead animal.

He walks through the decayed squalor of the rooms until he finds the old bedroom. He stands beside what remains of the bed and drops the flowers as you would into an open grave.

Wiping his nose on his sleeve, he peers to one side suddenly, as if expecting to find her here.

"He'd've been fifty-one today."

Waits. Nothing.

"I know you can hear me."

He moves over to the window and peers through a broken pane.

"I'd been alone since the day of his crash. But we were alone together, you and me. We had each other, didn't we?"

He rubs at his face. The scratch of bristle.

"I always loved him, you know. As if he were my own. And it didn't matter to me because you were so content..."

Pauses. Sniffs his fingers.

"Even though you always knew I knew."

The sound of a shotgun discharging in the nearby woodland makes him jump and grab himself, breaking the soliloquy.

Later, he stands on the moor again, staring at the pub in the distance. Sighs. Turns. Heads home.

Sheila is poised on the garden path outside his small, detached cottage, built from local stone. Curtains drawn. Overgrown garden. Looks like nobody lives here.

There are a couple of shopping bags at Sheila's feet. Her face says she's been unpleasantly surprised by life too many times and she is hoping this time will be different.

"Look," she says, "I don't mean to intrude, pet. Just let me make a start on that kitchen, eh? Get a proper meal inside you. You look like starvation."

She smiles, more confident now.

"I make a mean shepherd's pie."

Searching his face for any intimation of hostility, but he looks preoccupied.

"Howay. What do you say?"

He opens his mouth, as if to say a flat 'no', but then looks behind him, over the moor, and then up into the sky.

"Yon cloud..."

Finally he meets her eye.

"Yesterday..."

She shakes her head. "Forget it."

He holds her gaze for what feels like the longest time. "Door's open."

She smiles; he smiles.

He steps towards her and picks up the carrier bags.

She opens the front door and steps inside.

He stands in the doorway for a moment, staring out over the moor. Edith's perfect knowledge of him, from beyond the grave, has passed. But he sees his hardscrabble childhood on the farm, the way his father would look into the rhyme of his face and hated what he saw: his own weaknesses, his failings; sees Edith standing at the factory gates, waiting for him, still a girl with hope in her heart, sees the grief etched into her face as they watched William's coffin lowered into the ground while in the distance, William's blood father stood beneath the shade of a sycamore.

A rumble in the distance. Storm coming over the hills.

He reaches into his pocket to remove something. Expressionless, he examines the object in his hand and then places it on the stone lintel of the windowsill.

The jar of jojoba hand lotion.

He steps into the house, kicking the door shut behind him.

The Back Road
Reen Jones

When Mam died, it was a social worker who told me what had
happened. A 'bloody do-gooder', my Dad would have said. She
told me, quite matter-of-factly, as though it happened every day,
that Mam had been hit by a car while she was out shopping, and
she died straight away. Dad was working away from home at the
time, so I stayed two nights with a foster mother, then a different
social worker collected me. She tried really hard to be kind.

I sat hunched up on the back seat of her tiny car, staring
through the window with my teddy bear, a packet of sandwiches
and my few clothes in somebody else's battered suitcase. It was
winter and it rained all the way. I was being taken from my home
in London, where I had been born and had lived for my entire
seven years, to live with my Nan in Cefncoed, a small village in
South Wales; a foreign country I only visited for holidays. And
I knew that the Welsh side of my family hated my Dad, and
thought that whatever had happened, my Mam had brought it
on herself by marrying him.

Eventually, I fell asleep to the rhythm of the windscreen
wipers. When I woke up, we were just negotiating the last mile
or so of a single-track lane. The sky was thick, heavy, an angry
purple. Tar black trees overhung the road, swaying in the wind
like monsters reaching out to grab me.

Nan had obviously had to prepare things in a hurry. The spare
room was cluttered with boxes and piles of old newspapers, and

there was still a litter tray in the corner for the cat. I knew that I had stayed there before, but I couldn't remember how long ago. I wanted Nan to talk to me – tell me Mam was in heaven with Jesus, or something, but she gave me cocoa and toast with jam on and put me straight to bed. I cried, because I wanted to go home, but I no longer had a home to go to.

The next morning, things looked better. The rain had stopped and the sun was shining. We had breakfast, then I helped Nan in the house for a while, starting with feeding the cat, whose name was Smudge. He was a huge, black and white monster with a tummy that was always ready for tickling. I fetched in the milk and loaded sheets into the washing machine. That finished, I went out to explore the garden. Nan didn't mention Mam's death, or say how long I would be staying, and I didn't feel I could ask. I see now that she, too, was hurting inside.

The garden was massive, at least compared with what I was used to in London. Just outside the kitchen door, was a small neat patio where Nan grew herbs and big pots of geraniums: brilliant reds, oranges and pinks would burst into life in the spring. Further away from the house the garden became more wild and overgrown, until it finally ended in thick swathes of untended brambles. They had even started to encroach on the small gate which opened out onto the narrow road, that we had come up the night before. Locals just called it 'the Back Road'.

I didn't miss London. Whenever Mam got behind with the rent, we had to move house, and three different schools in as many years didn't make it easy for a quiet introverted child to make friends. When I saw a small girl about my own age walking across the field over the other side of the road, I eagerly asked Nan who she was. Nan looked puzzled. "There's no other little girls around here, Lyndie," she said, "the nearest house is about two miles away, and they don't have any children. Perhaps she's a holiday maker..."

Next time I saw her she waved and came up to the fence. She was sort of delicate looking, pale skinned, with long, wispy, red hair in pigtails.

"What's your name?" she asked.

"Lyndie."

"That short for Lynda?"

"Yes."

"My name's Alexandra really, but my Mam calls me Sandie," she giggled. "I'm seven."

"So am I," I said.

"If we stand here, we'll see the fire engine," she told me. We stood watching for ages, but it never came. We had fun waiting, though, and I now had a new friend.

Later, I told Nan I'd seen the little girl again, but she wasn't impressed. "Don't bring her in here," she said, "she's probably a Gypsy!" Nan didn't like Gypsies. She told me they stole children, though I couldn't understand why, and they broke into people's houses too apparently, and they didn't pay taxes either. I thought living in a caravan sounded exciting. When I asked Sandie about it, she gave me a blank look. She lived in a house in Bryn Mawr, and she didn't know anything about caravans.

Sandie and I played together all summer. Sometimes I would cross the road into "her" field, and sometimes she would come into the garden, where Smudge would be sun bathing. She showed me her secret hiding places in the woods, where we watched parent birds bringing back food for their squawk-ing chicks. We always looked out for the fire engine, too, but it never came. She didn't come into the house, though. I knew Nan would stop me playing with her if I brought her home, so I never talked about her. Of course, Nan must have seen her.

In September, I started school in the village. I was disappointed that Sandie didn't go to the village school, she said she went to the school in Bryn Mawr. Nan told me Gypsy children don't go to school. They had to work. Then they got married at thirteen years old, and had a baby every year. Because of the darkening nights, by the time I had had my tea and fed Smudge, it was too dark to go out. Saturday was shopping in Bridgend, and Sunday was chapel, so I couldn't play with her for a while.

Dad sent Nan a card at Christmas. He was working away somewhere. I think there was a letter as well, but she just sniffed and ripped it into small pieces. I wanted to ask her about what he said, but I knew not to. Nan never liked Dad. He wasn't good enough for Mam, she said. But I loved my Dad and wondered why he didn't come and see me. He could stay outside, like Sandie, if Nan didn't want him in the house.

When springtime returned, the evenings got lighter and I could play outside again. The first evening I went up to the end of the garden, Sandie was already walking across the field to the Back Road, and by the time I reached her she was leaning on the five bar gate waiting for me. We waited for the fire engine, as had become our custom, and then ran off to play. There were now two horses in the field, but far away at the top. Although last year Sandie and I had been the same height, this year I was nearly an inch taller than she was. I hadn't really made any friends at my new school yet. Most of the children had formed their alliances already, and my London accent labelled me as an outsider, so Sandie was special.

One day when I was playing on my own, I met the lady who owned the horses and she told me their names: Bobby and Betsy, and let me stroke them. She and her husband owned a small farm called Ty Goch, but she rented this field for the horses because it had extra nice grass. Nan let me bring them an apple each, and it didn't take them long to learn to come up to me and say hello as soon as they saw me at the gate. Sandie didn't like the horses, or they didn't like her. Gypsies liked horses, because they pulled their caravans, but I knew she wasn't really a Gypsy. I suspected the horses didn't like her because she never brought them apples.

We spent the summer holidays roaming the fields, checking out animals, birds and flowers and trying to catch fish in the stream. Later in the year, there would be blackberries to pick, and our mouths and hands would be stained purple. As ever, the summer ended too soon, and I was back at school. But now that I knew the horse lady, I could help feed the horses at weekends. About Christmas time, Nan got a phone call that made her very upset. She slammed down the phone. "He's left it a bit late to want to do something about it now!" she said. I asked if it was Dad, and she muttered something in Welsh, Mam's language, spoken when she was little, forgotten after she met Dad. I didn't understand it, but I recognised one of the words: one that made God really cross if you said it. I wasn't sure how I felt about Dad now. Two years is a long time when it's a quarter of your life. I hadn't heard a word from him since Mam died. I was hurt and angry. Why had he never come to see me, or even written me a letter? I was not a baby; I was nine now, and perfectly capable of reading a letter and writing back, if I had an address. Although Nan did her best, there was no warmth in her. I never felt that she really wanted me there. Her child-rearing years were past, and she hadn't wanted to start again. But she was the only family I had.

I spent a lot of time with the horses in early spring, and even got to start riding Bobby. This was something I had never dreamed I would get a chance to do. There were riding places in London, but they were far too expensive. They charged you by the hour, and you had to wear special clothes, which the charity shops didn't sell.

Just after my birthday, Sandie turned up again. It was a particularly hot summer which seemed to go on forever, and we had so much to do. When I look back on these years I marvel at the freedom we had. Who nowadays would allow a nine year old to be out all day with a bag of fish paste sandwiches and a bottle of lemonade? We played in the fields and paddled in the stream, armed with jam-jars to contain the sparkling silver fishes, always that little bit too smart to get caught. And watched for fire engines, which I was beginning to think didn't exist. Sandie wasn't right about everything. She knew where the blackbirds nested, but she was wrong about fire engines coming up the Back Road. They never did.

September came round again. I had to go back to school. I accepted that I wouldn't see Sandie until next year. It was dark when I got home from school, and I could not play out. But that was OK. I fed the horses, and rode Bobby from time to time. Then came another phone call. This time Nan did not try to fob me off.

"Lyndie, you're a big girl now," she said, "it's time you knew what's going on."

Dad had not been working anywhere all this time – he had been in prison. Now he was out, apparently a totally reformed character with a job and a steady girlfriend. He wanted to see me with a view to taking me back to London. Social Services insisted he had rights, and deserved another chance. Nan said that he gave up those rights when he chose to become a career-criminal. She also said Patsy was far too young for him, and he didn't deserve to have a child anyway. Social Services won, of course. So Dad and Patsy visited a few times, and so did the social workers, who kept asking me questions that started with, "How do you feel about . . .?". They never listened to the answers properly, and it was decided I should go back to London after Christmas.

It was meant to be a surprise when Dad and Patsy turned up a couple of days before Christmas. It was snowing when they arrived, the back seat of the car stacked high with presents for me and Nan, plus the biggest turkey I had ever seen. But Nan was embarrassed because she hadn't got them anything, and I was upset when I realised I wouldn't be able to see Sandie and might never see her again.

Nan had reluctantly put up a few decorations, and a very small Christmas tree in the window. Patsy told me about the tree they had in London, which would still be there when we got back. And, yes, I could have a kitten, and, yes, we could find one the same colour as Smudge. Nan was very quiet. She didn't get many visitors.

On Christmas Eve I went to bed early. Of course, I couldn't sleep. Sometime after midnight I got up to make sure it was still snowing. I pulled back my curtains. The path to the Back Road was covered so thickly you couldn't distinguish it from the garden. I had never seen snow like it before. Far away in the distance I could see a flashing blue light. I watched it come closer and closer. By the time it reached the bottom of the Back Road, I could hear the sirens and I knew what it was. It was the fire engine.

I didn't bother with my dressing gown, I just ran down stairs and threw open the back door. The fire engine was struggling up the hill through the rapidly freezing snow and it was too dark to see the firemen. But it was Christmas morning, and I had seen the fire engine! It was like an extra special Christmas present. I wondered if it was going as far as Bryn Mawr, and if Sandie would see it. There were no mobile phones in those days. I watched the flashing blue light until it disappeared into the woods. Sandie! Sandie! Look out the window. You were right all along!

Less than a week later, in the dead days between Boxing Day and New Year, I was in London with Dad and Patsy, for better or worse. I got my kitten, and we called him 'Smudge', but I had never got to say goodbye to Sandie, and I didn't know her address. Dad and Nan phoned each other a few times, but it didn't last. Nan told me she'd seen Sandie waiting by the gate a few times and I asked her to tell her I'd gone back to London. She said she'd tried to catch her, but by the time she got up the path, Sandie had gone.

Eventually, I left school, married someone unsuitable, divorced - I was never any good at the relationship thing. Some years later I heard that Nan had died. I was sorry and wished we had kept in touch. She probably did love me, in her way. After my marriage ended, I threw myself into my work for a while. But there were too many bad memories. I needed to move on, to get my life back. I decided to leave London and go back to the country, and started checking out 'Properties for Sale' ads. Then I saw it: Ty Goch, the horse lady's farm, was for sale.

I made an appointment, booked a B&B, and drove to Wales the following weekend. I wondered if I would see Sandie. I wondered what she had made of her life. Had she married, had children? I hoped she been happier than me.

Not a lot had changed. Nan's old house was still there, now belonging to strangers, of course. The brambles had all been cut down, but the gate to the Back Road was still as I remembered it. Everything looked smaller and less exciting now. Perhaps that's part of growing up and happens to everybody. The horse lady remembered me.

"You're Maggie's grand-daughter! Of course I remember you. You used to feed the horses."

She was delighted to see me as a prospective buyer, and showed me around the farm. She was widowed, and hoping to move out to Australia to live with her son. I asked her about Sandie. Did she remember her?

"Sandie? That little ginger girl from Bryn Mawr? Yes … Lloyd, I think her name was … Of course, I remember her. She died in that fire, isn't it? All her family were killed. It was terrible … I remember it as though it was yesterday. The fire engine had to come from Bridgend, you see. We'd had all that awful snow and the Back Road was blocked. They couldn't get through to Bryn Mawr. All of them, burnt to death. Tragic, it was." She paused for a moment, as though she had just remembered something. "But that was before you moved down from London. You wouldn't have known her."

"No. That's not right," I protested. "I played with her for three years. Even after I'd gone back to London, my Nan told me she had seen her waiting for me. I remember asking her to go out and speak to Sandie, but she always disappeared before Nan could get up there. She kept coming back for a few months, then she seemed to have given up. The fire must have been later."

The horse lady shook her head. "I don't think so. It was big news down here at the time. The enquiry and all that. It was in the South Wales Echo. Went on for weeks."

"What do you mean?"

"It turned out the little girl started the fire herself. They found a petrol can in her bedroom. I know she had problems at home. They always said in the village that her uncle used to bother her. Who knows what happens behind closed doors? Perhaps she was just bored and never meant it to spread like it did. Who's to say?"

"Perhaps she just wanted to see the fire engine," I said.

It was beginning to get dark when I left the farm. I told the horse lady I would be in touch, but I had already decided that I wouldn't be coming back. I got into my car and drove along the Back Road for the last time, past the field where the horses had been, heading for London where I now belonged. As I reached the five bar gate, opposite Nan's old house, I slowed down for one last look. But I didn't stop. In the distance I could already see a small figure, perhaps seven years old, with brilliant red hair, walking slowly across the field towards the gate, still watching for that fire engine that couldn't get up the Back Road.

A Dark Harvest
J. T. Seate

As a boy, I'd enjoyed roving through the knee-high weeds to the oldest stones in the cemetery, wondering if Indians had killed any of the deceased. The infant graves with lambs carved into the stones reminded me of how tough it was for people in olden times, but the place had never scared me, not until this night.

I was fourteen and my sister, Rachael, was twelve when we visited my grandparents during harvest season; on Halloween to be exact. My parents and we two kids lived in Dallas, but we had a passel of relatives who lived outside a little town in the hill country of Texas where the cemetery was. Two of our cousins, their parents, and our ailing grandparents lived together in a farmhouse. Haywood was a year older than me, and Barbara was my age, making Rachael the baby of the group.

Grandpa was bedridden and his memory wasn't worth a fiddler's fart. "God could punch his ticket at any time," my Mom used to say. Grandma's health was equally dubious making it hard for Uncle Ernest and his clan to keep the farm going while dealing with two invalids.

We arrived in the late afternoon. We paid our respects to grandpa, who looked no better than death warmed over, and to grandma who didn't look much better. We kids were then summarily shooed out of the house and shuffled over to a copse of trees. We found places to sit and watched the sun go down and a three-quarter moon rise. Haywood picked up a piece of tree limb and started whittling.

The two farm kids always enjoyed their little pranks when we city kids came for a visit. Barbara told Rachael and me about how they'd uprooted a few scarecrows and tipped a few pieces of light machinery the previous Halloween, the same as previous country generations had done.

"C'mon, Russ," Haywood said to me. "You got any ideas for later?"

"I don't feel like anything destructive," I answered. "Not with grandma being sick and all. How about we just go trick-or-treating?"

"Not many places in walking distance. You know that."

"I want to hear some ghost stories," Rachael said hopefully.

We watched the orange fireball change to a golden glow in the west while Haywood whittled his tree branch into a point. "We can make a few of these here stakes and go vampire-hunting."

"What ghost stories do you know?" Barbara asked me.

"You know the one about the Monkey's Paw?"

"Yeah, we read that in school," Haywood said, sounding bored.

"I never heard it," Rachael exclaimed.

"It's just about this guy who wishes his kid was alive and he uses up the other wishes trying to get him dead again," Haywood told her.

"How about old hook-arm?" I asked.

"There's a man down the road who fought in the war. He has one of those hooks that opens up," Barbara chimed in. "I hear he can't wipe his ass for shit."

"This is about a couple of kids that go to Lover's Lane and..."

"He feels her up and screws her blind?" said Haywood.

"Let Russ tell it," Barbara chided.

"So this couple is making out and they hear on the radio that

108

a guy with a hook arm has escaped from a mental institution and he's a mass murderer. So the girl gets all scared and wants to go home. The boy is pissed, but he hits the gas and takes her home. When the guy gets out of the car and comes around to get her out, he sees a hook dangling off his rear bumper."

"Like, they just pulled away in time, I guess," Rachael said.

"That's the idea."

"That's kinda scary," she added. "Do you have any stories, Haywood?"

Haywood stuck his carved stake into the ground. "I've got a heck of an idea. Let's go to the cemetery. You two have never been there at night, I bet."

"Don't you think we're a little old for that?" I said.

"I'm almost a teenager, for crying out loud," Rachael said to me, "and I think it would be cool."

"There you go," Haywood replied. "Here's what we'll do: make us some stakes, one for everybody. If we cut though the fields, the graveyard's just a mile."

"So, what'll we do when we get there?" I asked. "I don't want to knock over any gravestones."

"We'll write our names on the stakes. Each one of us will walk across the graveyard alone. When we get to the other side, we'll put our stake in the ground and come back. When everyone's gone across, we'll go over together and see if anybody chickened out. If your stake isn't there, then you cheated." Haywood looked at me. "You're not too pussy for that are you?"

I looked at Rachael, unsure whether her expression was one of expectation or something more like, "What are we getting ourselves into?"

"Mom won't let us go," she said.

"Your mom won't know." Haywood held up his stake, turning it around, admiring it. "They'll bed us guys down in the living room and you girls in one bedroom. We'll sneak out after they're asleep. Besides, it'll be creepier if it's real late."

So it was decided. Our cousins had their own pocket-knives so they whittled four large stakes.

"Let's don't make 'em too sharp," I cautioned, "in case somebody trips or something."

Haywood looked at me like I was a total nimrod city kid, afraid of his shadow. But I was only afraid of things that could really hurt you, not the graveyard, at least not then.

Around ten o'clock, the girls were shuffled off to their bedroom while we boys had the luxury of two living room couches. Haywood and I talked in hushed tones until my uncle hollered for us to go to sleep. For the next two hours I listened to the old house settle and a duet between my grandfather and a night owl. Granddad's breathing was so laboured I halfway expected the sound to suddenly stop, for him to die in the room on the other side of the kitchen.

I pictured him being lowered into the earth beneath the double stone that Grandpa and Grandma's sons and daughters had bought for them, their information already chiseled in except for the dates of death. I shivered at the thought of a stone awaiting my parents or even me and Rachael someday.

A trip to the cemetery didn't seem like such a great idea. I hoped everyone would forget the whole thing when a sudden absolute stillness stirred me. Granddad had stopped breathing. I wondered if I should wake someone, but then I heard him mumbling; some old saying, or maybe it was a song. I listened a while longer before closing my eyes. Something made me open them again. Hovering above me was Haywood's long face lit only by the light filtering through the window. His arm was poised above his head. He held a stake, ready to plunge it deep into my chest, or maybe into one of my eye sockets.

"Jesus," I said, and put up my hand in defense.

"Shhh." Haywood hissed, the sound cutting through the air

like a reaper's scythe. "Take it easy, you fairy. You'll wake some-body up. I'm just messin' with ya."

I wasn't convinced until he lowered his arm and replaced that maniacal grin with a less weird expression. "Maybe we should just get some sleep, Haywood."

"Don't be an ass-wipe. I'm gonna get the girls."

"But Grandpa..."

"Yeah, he does that a lot. Sings in his sleep. Put your shoes on."

The bedsprings squeaked like stepped-on mice while I grudg-ingly laced up my tennis shoes. When the girls entered the room, poor Rachael was yawning. I wished we could forget about our little adventure. The girls were dressed in long nightgowns that flowed down their forms like liquid moonlight. The gown must have embarrassed my sister, but she was determined not to com-plain about what inconveniences had to be endured at Grandma's house.

We left through the front door, careful not to make it squeak and we didn't speak until we were a good hundred yards from the house. The temperature was pleasant and didn't afford a reason to call this thing off. I'd never felt overly protective of Rachael, but on this night, she looked tired and fragile.

Haywood soon set the stage, lest we forget it was Halloween. "I'm following you," he moaned in a ridiculous baritone voice. "I'm getting closer...closer. Gotcha!" he said as Barbara grabbed Rachael from behind.

She let out a squeal, to their delight. "Don't do that, darn it," she protested and drew her arm back like she might hit Barbara, but then she laughed.

Long fingers of a cloud in front of the moon cast ominous shadows as the four of us trundled a quarter-mile through a har-vested field, complete with a menacing scarecrow. I half expected the ugly thing to raise an arm or shake a leg as we passed, serving as a warning of something more dangerous further along.

Eventually we were safely through the field and two barbed wire fences. The moon continued to shine fitfully through the scattered clouds illuminating our path. For a moment, I thought I saw a distant light up the gravel road leading to the cemetery.

"Did you see that?" I asked the others, but it had already winked out.

"Maybe the Headless Horseman," Haywood said.

"Maybe something else coming to play in the boneyard," Barbara suggested.

We walked on.

"Shhhh! Listen!" Haywood said.

We fell silent, the only sounds in our imaginations. Even the droning of the cicadas had stopped. I didn't like that.

"I thought I heard something, a chain rattling, maybe."

"Stop trying to scare us, Haywood," Rachael said.

He shrugged. "Isn't that what we're here for?"

Ahead was the infamous cemetery which held generations of corpses in silent, undisturbed repose. I hoped. It lay beyond the view of any farmhouses, waiting for us like a sentinel. We all fell quiet. Even Haywood's quips ceased as we made our way to the iron fence. On the other side were the oldest stones. They stood up like crooked teeth protruding from gums of uneven earth. The cemetery had plenty of stones with 19th century dates, but not many were fine enough to have soaring cherubs or grand guardian angels presiding over the deceased.

In the pale light, the rough rectangle of land looked like an evil oasis, an obstacle course with its high weeds, tombstones, a few modest crypts, all serving as barriers to be traversed.

We hunkered down in the dirt and scrub grass. I said, "Let's do it and get it over with." For me, Halloween, stories about things going bump in the night, and crossing the graveyard alone, had lost whatever shine it possessed when we were whittling

112

stakes and watching the sunset. "We should have at least brought a flashlight."

"Naw, the girls will be easy to see in their nightgowns," Haywood answered. "Besides, our eyes are adjusted to the light so if anyone decides to do something funny like hide behind a tombstone, we'll spot them."

"Nobody's gonna do anything like that unless it's you, Haywood," Barbara said.

"Okay," I said. "Let's make a pact right now that we didn't come all the way out here just to scare each other. Each person will walk across the place, stick their stake in the ground by the fence and come back."

"Who's first?" Haywood asked.

"It was your idea," his sister said. "You go."

"No problem." Haywood picked up one of the stakes, took a ballpoint pen from his pocket and wrote his name on its shaft.

"I'll see you scaredy-cats in about five minutes."

Haywood climbed over the black iron spears that had stood forever around the hallowed ground and I suddenly felt, no, I knew that we were violating some unwritten rule. I'd always heard of people doing ghoulish things in cemeteries at night. They robbed graves in some of the classic horror movies. I'd convinced myself I wasn't afraid of ghouls or ghosts or grave robbers, but I did feel we were tempting fate. I made up my mind that Rachael wasn't going to do this alone. I didn't care how much she protested.

I half way expected Haywood to try and scare us with a bloodcurdling scream once he was out of sight but, except for the girl's chatter, all was as quiet as… a graveyard.

Ten minutes passed, then fifteen.

"He's fuckin' with us," Barbara said.

It was the first time I'd heard a female use that word. I guess my surprise showed.

"Sorry. I'm kind of nasty sometimes away from home. I smoke too."

"That's all right. I..."

"BOO!" Haywood hollered, springing from the darkness."

I'm sure I levitated a foot. Rachael burst into tears.

"God damn it, Haywood!" Barbara yelled. "We said we wouldn't scare each other. Look, you got Rachael crying."

"Whoa, I didn't mean to scare you, Rachael."

"It's okay," Rachael sniffled. "I'm sorry for being so silly."

"No more of that crap or we're going back," I told Haywood.

He changed the subject. "Walking across is really a piece of cake. Just look out for a couple of footstones. They're hard to see. Almost broke my neck on one."

"I'll go next," I said. I wrote my name on my stake and clambered over the fence as Haywood had done. I just wanted to get it done and I was bolstered by the idea that years from now we'd all remember this crazy thing we did on Halloween.

I looked back only once. Twenty yards away the others were already fading from view. It was darker than I'd expected, darker than Haywood had let on. The wind picked that particular moment to pick up and whistle through the trees. The cloud cover had thickened. No wonder it was so hard to see.

About halfway across, I reminded myself that stone angels and dead bodies couldn't move, couldn't creep, couldn't talk. I looked to my left to where some of our ancient relatives were buried. Again, I thought I saw a glimmer of light, but it was beyond the cemetery up near the road. I tried to see until I heard the rustle of leaves. Something had moved.

I froze. A figure rose above a black gravestone directly ahead of me. Its body undulated and then it crawled to the side of the stone revealing its spiked pelt. It jumped down and scurried away in the dark. A goddamned porcupine.

Once I started to breathe again, I walked faster, not worrying about the footstones Haywood had warned about. I should have worried. Closing in on the fence, my toe caught something and I fell forward. One hand hit hard dirt clods and the other hit… nothing. I floundered for a moment and managed to shift my weight and roll away from the open pit.

Haywood didn't say there was an open grave. The bastard.

The grave had been dug recently. The hard clods of earth felt cold and smelled fresh. There was no stone and I was thankful I hadn't hit the hole dead-on. A broken leg would have been the best scenario, but more likely a cracked skull would have resulted.

I picked myself up, brushed myself off, and walked the rest of the way to the fence. I looked for Haywood's stake and realised each of us would take a different path and that it could be anywhere. He probably hadn't come as close to the open grave. I plunged my own stake into the ground and started back, careful to avoid the opening in the earth and equally careful not to run.

During the return trip, I thought I saw all manner of squirmy, creepy-crawlies on the stones and crypts. An angel with a broken wing crouched on a headstone like a gargoyle ready to spring. A mausoleum door looked to be ajar as the wind picked up to a nasty, sand-blowing whine. Suddenly, all the scary stories I'd heard over the years seemed real to me, the blood-suckers and monsters, the demons from hell and the escaped lunatics with hooks for hands. My teeth began to chatter. Rotting corpses were undoubtedly stirring from their long, dark sleep. I'd had all the graveyard adventure I wanted for one night.

"Over here," Barbara called.

I rejoined the group. "Do you know there's an open grave near the fence?" I said looking straight at Haywood.

"You have to be yanking my crank."

"There's an open grave. I almost fell in. It's not safe for anyone else to go in the dark."

"You sure you don't have bats in your belfry?" Haywood said, but without much conviction. "I didn't hear about anybody dying around here."

"Maybe it's somebody from town. Who knows, but it's there."

"The rest of you want to go home?" Haywood asked.

"I want to go across," Barbara said pushing out what chest she had in bravado. That must have played well with the country types. "After I get back, we'll leave."

Rachael didn't protest. "Why do you want to go, Barb?" she asked.

"I just want to prove I can do it."

"Stay over to the left in the direction of the family graves and you'll be away from the hole," I said. "When you get back, we'll all split. Right?"

Everyone nodded. Rachael looked like she could fall asleep standing up so I knew she wouldn't unload on me for not getting her turn.

Barbara picked up a stake. "Guess I don't need to write on it if we're not doing a stake-check. If I'm not back in fifteen, send in the Marines." She looked like an apparition, floating over the ground in her long nightgown.

Black clouds were swept over the sky by an ethereal wind. I'm not sure how long we waited for Barbara to come back. One minute can seem like ten when you're waiting for something, and by then we were chilled and thirsty.

"Do you think Barb's messin' with us to get even with me?" Haywood asked.

"Dunno. She's your sister."

"I'm going after her," he said.

Before I could object, Haywood clambered over the fence and ran into the dark. His hair and his shirt tail blew eastward as he disappeared from sight. Several more minutes passed. A scream tore through the night like something out of a horror movie. It almost sounded like the bay of Lon Chaney's werewolf.

Then, "Help!"

"Russ, go check," Rachael pleaded.

"Promise you'll stay right here."

"Yes," she promised, truly frightened.

I headed back along the path. Haywood was just ahead, kneeling over something. Barbara lay on the ground next to the fence.

"I don't think she's breathing," Haywood wailed. "She's…"

I knelt down next to them and put my head on Barbara's chest, not sure if I was hearing anything. I shook her shoulders not knowing what else to do.

"She's dead!" Haywood cried.

I guess I sort of went into shock. I looked at Barbara's gown. It stretched to the foot of the fence. Her stake was driven through the hem.

"Oh lord. Oh, good lord." She must've been spooked. In her haste to get back she drove the stake through her nightgown. When she turned to leave, it pulled taut. She thought something was grabbing her. Can someone be scared to death, I wondered?

"Check her pulse or something," Haywood urged.

I looked at her once more not wanting to touch her, not wanting to be next to something dead.

"Please," Haywood pleaded.

I touched her wrist, hoping to feel a pulse. "Please, Barb, please."

Her eyes flew open. She made a horrible, guttural sound like the bride of Dracula. I stumbled back and grabbed Haywood's legs. An indefinable sound came from my mouth as I struggled to get to my feet. Barbara rose up and reached for me.

Someone screamed then. It must have been me because Barbara's expression changed. She began to laugh. I looked up at Haywood. He broke into laughter and fell to the ground, his arms around his sides, his chortles coming in waves of delight.

I looked back at Barbara who'd lain back down, tears of

amusement streaming down her temples. The sound of their laughter surrounded me.

"You should've seen your face," Haywood managed to choke out. "You looked like you'd seen..." He couldn't continue, rolling in the dirt, holding his sides, yucking it up.

"City boy, city boy," Barbara hooted. "We didn't mean to give you a heart attack. Can you talk?" she said, her glee subsiding somewhat.

I stood up. "Were you planning this all along?"

"Just when you went across. Me 'n' Haywood decided the night was too boring." She was now at the giggle stage.

"Hook, line and sinker," Haywood added, his chuckles slowing, revelling in their success.

I walked to the fence and pulled Barbara's stake from the ground. I looked it over while their fits of laughter became intermittent. I thought about attacking them with the stake, acting like they'd driven me mad, but what was the point in being equally juvenile? They had gotten me good and that's all there was to it.

"Where's Rachael?" Barbara asked.

"I left her on account of you two." I started back, leaving them behind.

"Hey," Barbara called. "Wait up. Don't be mad."

"Think of how we'll all have a good laugh later about gettin' ole city-boy a good one."

"Stop it, Haywood," Barbara said quietly. "That's enough."

I returned as quickly as I could, not wanting Rachael to be alone and at the same time wondering if she'd heard the cousins plotting their little scheme to nail me. If so, I probably wouldn't speak to her for some time, but I didn't really believe she would have gone along with it.

I'll never know, because when I got back, Rachael was gone.

"What's the deal now?" I said. "You guys tell Rachael to hide?"

"No, I swear," Barbara said, as mystified as I was.

Then I saw something on the far side of the fence, Rachael's clothes, her borrowed nightgown and her underwear stacked in a neat little pile on top of her tennis shoes.

"Rachael!" I called.

Haywood and Barbara joined in. "Rachael! Rachael! Come on!"

I gathered up the clothes and ran back the way we had come toward the farmhouse. I prayed that this was another elaborate hoax. I was responsible for my little sister, but I'd left her alone. I prayed she would be at the house waiting for us. That has to be it I thought, she was scared and decided to come back by herself. It would sure give us a scare, me most of all, a lot better than what the cousins had pulled. But as hard as I tried to believe it, I couldn't picture my twelve-year-old sister running through the countryside naked, with no shoes.

The Devil had her, making me pay for my negligence. With my heart hammering fit to break free of my chest, I ran all the way to the house.

Everyone was up. "Is Rachael here?" I almost screamed.

They all looked at me queerly.

"Where have you been?" my mother asked.

I stood there clasping Rachael's clothes against my chest wondering what else had happened.

"Your grandmother passed away during the night, Russell." She fought back tears. "Where is everyone?"

I could hear my grandfather singing a tune in the bedroom. At that moment, it seemed to me that the whole world had gone insane.

When the other two arrived, I sat on the couch with my head in my hands and told both sets of parents the whole story. I waited for Haywood or Barbara to say it was their fault, but they never did, the shits. My uncle Ernest was on the phone the moment I'd finished.

They searched for days, local people and State Troopers. I kept thinking about that screaming mouth of earth I'd nearly fallen into, the empty grave. An old man of ninety was laid to rest that morning, the day the search began. I hoped someone had crawled down in that hole before the burial to make absolutely sure nothing had been buried deeper down.

People stopped searching long enough to witness Grandma's interment four days later. Two days after that, Grandpa croaked. The remaining sons, daughters, grandsons and granddaughters came to pay their respects to Grandma and hung around for Grandpa's funeral. The little country cemetery had a busy week. One bible-beating relative had the audacity to proclaim that Rachael had been taken up to be with her grandparents. Frighteningly, some authorities thought that as good an explanation as any.

I didn't go to the services. I never went near that graveyard again because I was afraid I might hear Rachael calling for help, calling for me to find her. If I'd had three wishes on a monkey's paw, they would have been that no one had died, no one went missing, and no one had gone to that damned cemetery.

Weeks later, I remembered something no one else had thought about: the unused stake. It was missing when I came back to the fence, vanished into thin air just like Rachael. Things were never the same between my family and my cousins, nor between my parents and me. Even though they never accused me, I served a penance for my role in Rachael's disappearance. In fact, life has been a struggle because my memories all return to that Halloween night. We all lost something we could never get back, until now.

If the party or parties responsible for my sister's disappearance read this, I beg you to take pity and tell me exactly what happened. I know you're out there. I know because of what I found in my mailbox yesterday: an old, weathered stake with the letters R-a-c-h-a-e-l crudely scrawled on its shaft.

A Clean Slate
Fran Hill

I put the letter back inside the envelope so that the words could not watch me and placed it on my dressing table. I dragged a chair and stood on it to pull a leather suitcase from the top of the wardrobe. Dust clouded up as I slid it to the edge. I stepped down, laid the suitcase on the bed and opened it.

The purple silk inside was faded in places, and nestling in a fold in the corner of the case was a pearl drop earring. It was the one I had lost two years ago during our holiday in Florence. We had spent ages hunting for it, bumping heads as we swept our arms under the bed in the search, and laughing, and kissing. We'd had to rush to catch the plane back to England, leaping into taxis, oblivious to other people and their lives.

Now I cupped the earring in my hand and, as I looked at it, I recalled how it had been then.

I picked out the earring's partner from an ivory box on my dressing table. Pushing out the silver studs from my pierced ears, I replaced them with the pearls. I stroked the smooth opaque tear-shaped drops with finger and thumb, remembering. I looked in the mirror. That summer in Florence my skin had been brown and glowing and my eyes content, but the pearls now looked dirty and incongruous against my strained white face, so I tugged them out and threw them into a corner of the room. Against the green of the carpet they looked clean again. So it was just me.

That's what he always said these days: "Things wouldn't be so bad if you were different."

A breeze nipped in through the open window and the thin curtain fluttered over my dressing table. The cream envelope slid off the polished surface and onto the floor at my feet. I placed my foot on top of it so I could not see the writing on the front and swept it backwards and forwards across the carpet underneath my foot. It went sssh-sshh-sshh as it moved along the pile, a gentle rhythm like tiny stones in a rain stick.

I left the letter under the bed.

Opening the door of the wardrobe, I ran my hands along the rows of dresses, skirts and blouses. Which should I take? Lifting out my green dress, I laid it on the suitcase, folding the skirt up towards the lace-edged neck, tucking it in at the sides, bending to stroke it tidy.

I stood up, furious. This was how I had packed for Italy, loving and caring for each garment. What did it matter now? What did any of it matter? I grabbed clothes – any clothes - from the wardrobe, hauled them across to the bed and flung them inside the case. I squashed them down then turned back for more. Faster and faster I worked, sweeping shoes out from the floor of the wardrobe and throwing them in on top of soft blouses, my vision misted by tears.

I pulled shut the lid and leaned on it hard to lock the case.

Spent, I sat on the bed and bent down to retrieve the letter. I had read it a hundred times since it had dropped oh so light and oh so innocent onto the doormat that morning. I inched the folded paper out of the envelope, thinking that, like a child's Magic Slate, the writing might disappear and leave a clean sheet. But the small, flowing handwriting was still there, elegant and polite. Where were the thick, black letters that usually yelled out such news? Why were there not scraps of newspaper stuck in a mosaic of menace? I took a deep breath and exhaled, pushing the pain of it deep inside me, low down where it couldn't escape.

Not yet.

I slipped the letter into the pocket of my skirt and walked downstairs, holding onto the banisters, as frail as an old woman, as though my bones would splinter if I tripped. The stairs seemed steep, each step an effort. I felt for footholds.

I walked through to the kitchen; the rooms were cold and unfriendly, like an empty church on a winter Saturday.

The kitchen clock tick-tocked as I looked out of the window onto the long garden. Louder it ticked, and it began to chant, echoing the words in the letter. I gripped the edge of the sink, trying to block out the taunts, but they kept on coming and they wouldn't stop, so I reached up, unhooked the clock and hurled it out of the kitchen window onto the patio. It lay face down among pots of herbs, like a drunken man who falls in a pretty garden on the way home. I slammed the window shut and pressed my hands over my ears until the ticking subsided.

I began to cook his dinner.

I heard the sound of his key and stood very still, my hand in my pocket. The door closed. I listened to his measured footsteps on the parquet floor of the hall.

He opened the door to the dining room. I heard his briefcase being laid on a chair, a click, and then the rustle and snap of his newspaper. This was how it had been lately. He never came into the kitchen now, but sat at the dining room table to wait. When had he last surprised me by stealing into the kitchen, putting his hands over my eyes, snuggling into the back of my neck, caressing the tops of my arms as I ladled soup into deep bowls?

When I walked in with the tray, he was smoothing his hands over the white tablecloth, trying to flatten the creases I always ironed in. I waited as he rearranged a vase of flowers so that it sat over a small gravy stain on the cotton. I wondered how I had ever laughed at this.

124

I placed his meal on the table in front of him. I sat opposite and watched. I watched as he ate the meal I had cooked for him.

"Nice steak." Those were his words of greeting. He put down his knife and sipped his wine. "Not eating?" He raised his eyebrows. I made no comment, just shrugged. I studied him as, efficiently, he slid the serrated knife into the tender sirloin, as he speared the meat with his fork, stabbed at a button mushroom and raised the food to his mouth. The sound of his chewing was regular; he was business-like when he ate. More murmurs of appreciation, more wine, more meat, more mushroom.

He wiped clean his plate with a last piece of fried potato, arranged the cutlery side by side on the plate, patted his stomach and leaned back in the chair. I poured him some more wine. The room was hot, the heavy curtains drawn together. The dark maroon wallpaper seemed to bring the walls in so close. I wanted to spread my arms, pushing back the walls like Samson before they crushed both of us.

His eyes caught mine.

"Not hungry?" he said. Another two word sentence. He spoke sparingly, wasting no breath, no effort on me. In my mind I saw a picture of him, his face softened by the warm amber of a candle in an Italian restaurant. Then, he had leaned towards me, reached for my hand across the table, and we had smiled and whispered and talked of everything and nothing.

I lifted my hand to feel the pearls in my ears but remembered that they lay abandoned in a corner of the bedroom. I had not put my studs back in and felt exposed without them.

In the heavy silence, my eyes focussed on the white octagonal plate in front of him, traces of red from the rare steak smearing the chaste china.

"Good day?" he asked. I watched him. His brow furrowed and his gaze dotted around the room, as though looking for clues. He searched the walls and lifted his eyes to study the light shade above the table. I could see the walls drawing in fast but I don't think he knew. He shifted in his chair, and picked up his glass again. His eyes were narrowed over the crystal. Not for months had he examined me so closely.

"I had a letter today," I said. My eyes did not leave his.

"Oh," he laughed, but there was doubt. "What, a proper letter? Not a bill?" It was a joke and it was seven words but it was too late for amusement and too late for conversation. My hands were damp and warm and I ran them down my skirt. I could hear the faint rustle of the letter in my pocket. His eyebrows lifted again, and I think he heard the sound of the paper. He didn't ask if he could see it.

He did not speak for a while, but I could still hear the walls approaching and there was a rainstorm in my ears. I wondered if I had screamed but he didn't look shocked, just apprehensive. He began to fold his napkin, smoothing the already smooth linen, halving it, quartering it.

"It's happening again, then." I think it was me that was speaking, but my voice seemed to come from somewhere outside the walls, outside the world.

"Happening again?"

I pushed the letter along the tablecloth towards his plate. He looked down at it but didn't move. The silence hammered at my mind and I flinched as the hot, red wallpaper began to curl off the walls in thick sheets and cave in towards us. Bile rose in my throat and he and his chair were falling, clumsy and heavy, onto the thick pile of the Turkish carpet.

His blood mingled with beef blood on the plate, and stained the tablecloth.

I rearranged his cutlery neatly and bent to straighten his tie so he wouldn't be found dishevelled. As the rumble of falling brickwork grew and crashed in my head, I ran upstairs to fetch my suitcase, closing the dining room door behind me so I could never be blamed for dust in the hallway.

Mrs Jones' House
Scotty Clark

Looking back on 1974, I've never known a freedom like it, nor felt so free in my actions, so immune from consequences. I only wish I'd been old enough to recognise it there and then, because I would have revelled in it. Nottingham City Council was slum-clearing the Meadows, which had been deemed unfit for human habitation. Entire streets were emptied of life and awaited demo-lition. Communities were moved en masse to the newly-built St. Ann's and Clifton estates. Lots of my friends went to Clifton but my family moved to St Ann's as it was like the Meadows: a pub on every corner. My Dad liked a pint.

It was a Sunday in October. Goose Fair had been and gone, and the goldfish that we'd won at Hook-A-Duck was already dead. They never lasted long. Some blamed the chlorine in the water, but the truth was that it was me playing with it as if it was a hamster. The winter chill arrived in the autumn that year but we'd been basking in the newly discovered joy of central heating, sweating it out in the luxury of inside toilets and soaking in baths full of hot water. No longer did we need to go to Portland swim-ming baths for a wash. But that all came to an end when the first gas bill arrived and from then on we were forced to share each other's bathwater. Lots of families from our old street had been moved onto the same new street, so we knew loads of our neigh-bours. The McCall family who'd lived at the far end of our old street were now directly across the road from us, and my Mam was furious.

"Trust me to get them as neighbours! The good-for-nothing thieves they are. They'd nick the sugar out of your tea!" Without warning she grabbed me by the shoulder and sat me down on the sofa that was covered with suitcases full of clothes.

"You are forbidden from playing with them boys, do you hear me?" She shouted. I nodded.

"They're a bad bunch and you'll end up in trouble." She looked over her shoulder through the window that looked out towards their back garden, as if the McCall's were there watching.

"That Chris McCall's been taking boys down playing in the old houses, and one of them fell through floorboards and died, do you hear me?" I nodded.

"Promise me you won't go into those houses?"

"I promise."

She gave me a quick hug then sent me upstairs with bags of clothes.

I could see Chris McCall from my bedroom in his back-garden; he'd be dropping boulders on unsuspecting snails or digging for worms and burning them with matches. He was the youngest of four brothers. They all had massive heads, were all equally deranged, and, like their Dad, were always in trouble with the police. Chris wasn't deformed but his head was much bigger than his brothers'. He had a shock of dense, black hair that stood up even when it was wet. His tabs stuck out like swollen baby's fists. His long crooked nose suddenly stopped like the tip of a snooker cue, and his buck teeth bulged out of his puckered mouth. His brothers had nicknamed him 'TNT' for his teeth, nose and tabs. He reckoned TNT was because of his explosive temper, but I knew differently.

Anyway, this chilly sunny Sunday morning, which saw Dad sleeping it off whilst my Mam and our Theresa had gone to morning Mass, McCall actually came a-knocking, asking if I wanted to go down to our old street. I looked at him trying not to stare at his tabs, nose and teeth.

"My Mam said I'm not allowed in them." I said. But really I was flattered and excited that he'd called for me.

"We're not going in them." he grinned, "We're only going to look at them." Mam wouldn't be back for at least an hour. I felt the lure of the excitement, the thrill of the forbidden.

"Come on she'll never know," he said turning on his heel. I picked my coat up and closed the door, simple as that.

He said Mam's story about the dead boy was just a story she'd invented to put me off going in them. I didn't know who to believe, I didn't want to get into trouble with my Mam and I didn't want to come across as chicken. I figured all I had to do was go along with him, and make sure Mam didn't find out. Anyway, as he said, we weren't going to go into the old houses, we were just going to look them.

We cut across Carlton Road and into Sneinton, past the derelict windmill, down Meadow Lane, and past a deserted Magpie pub, which used to be the community centre for the people who'd lived on the empty streets. It's hard to describe, the feeling of seeing the place where you were born and bred turned into a ghost town. Streets that once teemed with life now stood silent and forlorn, as if ashamed of their abandonment, silenced by corrugated iron sheeting nailed over doors and ground floor windows, like gaffer tape over the mouths of terrified hostages.

The demolition had already started. Houses that knew a century of secrets, sadness and celebrations were flattened reduced to broken bricks and fractured wood that stuck out at impossible angles. Rooms that had once been the most precious and private of sanctuaries, that witnessed births, deaths and conceptions, all gone, but for four walls of newly exposed wallpaper, two up and two down, like stamps on a parcel.

We walked down our old street in silence, past old Mrs. Jones' house, which was next in line for destruction when the demolition men returned the next day. With her long greasy grey hair pulled back, no teeth and oversized specs that fell off her nose, she'd stand on her doorstep on warm days in her shawl, or look out of her window on rainy or cold days. She wore stockings the colour of sticking plasters and those tiny fur lined boots with the zip up the front that all old women seemed to wear in those days. Today she'd be described as an eccentric, or at worst labelled as having learning difficulties, but that's just how she was. She loved children but never had any. She was always playing with the babies, talking to us kids, giving us sweets and biscuits. My Mum said that her husband had been like my Dad, a plasterer, and that he died young in WW1, and she'd been alone ever since. Many of us kids didn't have grandparents locally because our parents had come to England seeking a better life, and we looked upon her as a Granny. She soaked up the love; she was a Gran to multiple generations.

She refused to leave her house, the house she'd lived in all of her life. The council offered her a flat in the Meadows or St. Ann's, or a care-home: whatever she wanted. But what she wanted was to stay in her house to the very end, and stay she did, leaving in a coffin only last month. The whole street went to her funeral. It coincided with the last days of the Meadows and a big piss up in the Magpie: grown men crying at the thought of it all coming to a sad end, unsure of tomorrow, with a bellyful of ale at the funeral of a woman who had come to epitomise the community. It seemed right and proper that such men, who'd never shed a tear in public, did so now. "End of an era," they said. It felt like everybody's Granny's funeral. She was finally reunited with her husband and buried in the same plot she had secured for him so long ago.

As we turned into the back yards, I could see that all the

houses had had the corrugated iron sheeting ripped off and the kitchen doors crow-barred open. McCall returned from one of the coal sheds waving a large hammer around his head, a demented look on his face that I hadn't seen before. Running into the adjacent outside toilet he smashed the toilet bowl into pieces then destroyed two more in rapid succession. He stood there panting, with a huge grin on his face, before passing me the hammer. I gleefully ran to the next strip of outside toilets, kicking open the doors and smashed the lavatory pans into pieces with a wildness that dug deep at the heart of me, stirring a ferocious, feral freedom that I never knew existed. I stood there panting, eye-to-eye with McCall, who produced a bucket of coal. A trickle of blood ran from where a shard of shattered pottery had cut my face just under my eye. Passing me two black, shiny lumps of coal, McCall began smashing the upstairs windows. Sensing the freedom and impunity to destroy, I nurtured the beast within me, feeding its fury. I revelled in the sound of glass shattering, only stopping when I ran out of coal.

McCall came over and showed me a shiny, brand new fifty pence piece.

"My wages from me Dad, for helping strip the metal from them houses," he smiled, carrying on walking towards one of the boarded up doors.

"There's none left, we've got everything out last week." He said, putting the money back in his pocket, before disappearing behind a slice of corrugated sheeting that was still nailed to the door frame on one side, so it worked like a hinge.

"Come on then," he called from the other side of the sheeting. I twitched into life and followed. That was that, my big moment of disobeying my Mam.

We stood in a scullery with whitewashed walls, and tell-tale signs where McCall's Dad had liberated lead and copper piping.

Past the scullery door I could see the darkened living room where the only light cascaded from the staircase. We walked up the stairs where we found two sunlit rooms. One contained a chest of drawers, full of women's clothes. In my imagination it was pirate's clothing and I put on a black and white striped dress because it was Notts County's colours. At the bottom of the chest were woman's wigs and cheap jewellery which we also put on excitedly. We ran down the stairs in search of more pirate treasure, plunged back into the darkness and followed the light through the kitchen door.

All the houses were the same: two up, two downs, with an additional bedroom built over the scullery, which usually served as a nursery. Systematically, we ran through each room in each house. Some were totally empty, some still had beds, furniture and pictures on the walls as if the people had left in hurry or had bought new furniture for their new house, abandoning the old. Drawers of clothes and boxes of junk were opened and thrown around the rooms. Nowadays, some of it would fetch a pretty penny: clothing and items from the 1940's through to the mid 70's. We found a box of make-up and adorned our faces with tribal artwork. We must have looked like characters from The Lord of the Flies as we ran from room to room and house to house. We were wild, we were free, we were furious. Looking back I'm glad we didn't find any matches. We would have torched the houses, such was our spirit.

Chairs were thrown out of windows, wardrobes were pushed downstairs. In one house a wardrobe got stuck in the narrow stairwell, blocking our way out. We set about it, smashing it to splinters to get out and into the next house. We found wooden sticks which we carried like spears, looking in every room, search-ing for treasure. One room had a number of orphaned dolls which we kicked around like footballs until their heads came off. We stuck them onto our poles, like the heads of the vanquished dead and trouped off into the next house with our spoils of war. We were without limits or responsibilities: not a care in the world. As I said, I've never known anything like it since.

Mrs. Jones' house was the last remaining house of that terrace; the rest had been demolished. We were, for the first time in our adventure, acutely aware of whose home we were in. Mrs. Jones had recently died. It felt wrong to enter. It hadn't stopped McCall's Dad of course, who had clearly been in for the lead and the copper, leaving it open for the likes of us. As Mrs. Jones had no family her house had been emptied by the council clearance people. It still smelt the same: brown paper, biscuits and cooked cabbage. We walked into each room disappointed that there was nothing we could play with or throw out of the windows. For some reason McCall stared at the wall in the back bedroom lifting his head up and down, a confused look on his face.

"There's no little room." he said. I hadn't even noticed, but I followed him as he went running outside. True enough, like each and every house in those streets, it was a two up, two down with an extension: a scullery on the ground floor and a small room above with a dirty window and green curtains.

"There's a room there, look." He ran into a coal shed, returning with a rusting spade. To be honest, if he hadn't noticed, I would have just run up the alley to the back of the next row of terraces and carried on foraging.

We stood facing the wall where a door should be, staring at green flowers on faded white wallpaper, so smooth and flat. There was a bright, unsullied square where a mirror or framed print had hung for a lifetime. McCall tapped the wall, a hollow sound. He raised the shovel above his misshapen head and drew it down with all the force an eight year old, high on adrenaline, could muster. The shovel sank deep into the plaster, and we smiled. There was a secret space behind the wall. A few more blows and there was a hole big enough for both our heads. We looked but

134

the space behind the wall was in total darkness. I started to pull away the plaster, again McCall drove the shovel down, tearing at the wooden slats and soon we were standing in the room we'd found.

Light and fresh air poured into the room for the first time in many years. I could see thousands of tiny specks of dust ebbing and flowing like illuminated plankton. I could just make out a glowing, dim green rectangle of light. I took a cautious step forward. It was daylight coming through curtains. My mouth was dry and I coughed as I inhaled the dust. I tugged at the curtains and they fell to the floor, causing heavy chunks of dust to burst like puff balls. Muted daylight seeped through grimy windows, illuminating the room. I pulled at the window which opened with surprising ease, initiating a riptide through the plankton as fresh air spilled into the room. McCall was on his haunches looking at two chairs arranged face to face with a wooden box sitting on them. It was a very small coffin, about the size of a shoe box, covered in dust. McCall lifted the lid. We saw the tiny skeleton of a baby, surrounded in delicate, grey-white lace. I felt a deep and sudden fear grip my stomach and I made the sign of the cross. I looked around the room with dread. I'd seen vampire films on TV and I knew coffins and skeletons meant that Count Dracula wasn't far behind. I started crying; no longer a pirate pillaging ships, I was an eight year old wanting his Mam.

"We need to go… we need to tell a grown-up," I said as tears rinsed dust, blood and make up down my cheeks. McCall crouched down on all fours, almost nose to nose with the baby's skull. He extended his coal-blackened finger towards the skeleton but his hand twitched and he snatched it away. I saw the same demented look he had when he smashed half a dozen toilets. He clenched his fist, to punch the baby's head. I pulled him back, sending him off balance, falling onto his backside. He glared round at me furiously. I shook my head as I looked into his eyes, afraid that he would live up to his nickname with explosive anger.

"You can't hurt it, it's a wee baby," I sobbed. Something in him changed. He blinked as the perpetual dust settled on his eyelids. He nodded.

We ran onto the deserted, disappearing streets. I think we were expecting to find children playing, adults coming and going and Mrs. Jones on her doorstep. But the once familiar places were all abandoned houses and piles of rubble.

McCall pointed. "There's a phone box, we can call the Police." We could see the phone-box on Meadow Lane across the plains of debris. Bright red, it represented contact with the grown up world and we ran towards it. Like war-weary soldiers travelling through no man's land.

We stood panting in the phone-box, our breath condensing on the cold glass. We held the phone between our heads, like we were sharing the sounds of a sea shell. I dialled 999. The dial clicked and purred, and we were through and heard the Operator asking what we wanted.

"We've just found a baby in a coffin," I said, "In Mrs. Jones' house." She told us to stop wasting her time. McCall was incensed.

"Honest Missus! We're not lying! We've just found a baby in a coffin." The woman paused, and then her tone changed. She confirmed where we were and told us to stay by the phone box to wait for the police. It was getting dark, and I heard the wind whistle through a hole in one of the glass panels. We stepped outside. The galloping wind tore across the space the demolition had made, blowing a huge bruise of a sky that tumbled down towards the River Trent.

McCall heard it first, the wailing siren that got louder and louder. We saw a jam sandwich police-car speeding towards us. It screeched to a halt at the phone box. The sound of the siren was incredible and the copper must have seen me put my hands over

my ears because he turned it off. I could see the coppers looking
at each other as our story tumbled out. Before we knew it we
were in the back of the police car. They knew McCall well, knew
of his family, and McCall was proud of this. He sat smiling as we
neared Mrs. Jones' house. I don't think the policemen believed us,
not that they thought we were lying but rather, somehow mis-
taken.

The hole that we had made was too small for the coppers to
get through so they used the spade to make it big enough. Like
us, they coughed as the plankton-dust ebbed and flowed and the
hole got bigger. I remember the larger of the two cursing under
his breath, his black tunic streaked with chalk-grey plaster as he
squeezed through the hole. The demeanour of the policemen
changed when they saw the delicate, dust-covered baby skeleton.
They took us back to the car and radioed for assistance. A police-
woman and policeman arrived in another car. The woman had a
large bag of Liquorice Allsorts, and McCall ate the ones covered
in blue and pink coloured candy balls. I felt very special as they
drove us home, letting us eat all the Liquorice Allsorts.

The sight of a police car pulling up outside McCall's house
was enough to make his brothers quickly disappear. Through
the panels in our fence I could see my Mam washing up at the
kitchen sink. Her face changed as she looked up, saw the police
car and craned her neck to get a better view. I could see her lips
move and I knew she'd be cursing the McCall family. The police-
woman opened my door. As I got out I saw Mam's mouth flop
wide open. She stared at me for what seemed like ages, her mouth
wide-open like a biscuit barrel, then she twitched into action and
the back door burst open. She bounded down the back garden
path towards the gate. As she opened it she met the policewoman
who must have clocked the anger on Mam's face and the subse-
quent terror on mine, because she steered Mam away from me
and into the back-garden. Mam still had washing up bubbles on

the backs of her hands. I saw anger turn to shock as the Police-woman related the events of the day. Her face went as pale as the apron she gripped, when she heard of our find in one of the houses that she'd warned me not to go anywhere near.

Resembling a transvestite dwarf with acid inspired psychedelic face paint smeared with blood and tears, I looked at Mam who loomed over me. She smelt of Sunday dinner and I suddenly realised how hungry I was. I knew I was in big trouble. I'd promised her that I'd stay away from the old houses.

She scooped me up with strong arms and held me tightly. I could see tears in her eyes.

As I bathed in the extravagance of a deep bath of hot, bubbly water she extracted the full story from the moment McCall knocked on the door through until the police brought us home. Our Theresa knelt beside her on the new linoleum flooring. They both wept and blessed themselves several times as I described the moment we first set eyes on Baby Jones.

I became a minor celebrity and never tired of telling the story to strangers on the estate who would stop and ask me about it. The story spread like wildfire. There was a police investigation and I was interviewed several times, as was McCall. The inquiry found birth and death certificates but no funeral record for Baby Jones, who, as it transpired, was in fact a wee girl called Martha, born January 1916 and died four weeks later. The coroner's report suggested that Mr. and Mrs. Jones were so grief-stricken about the death of their daughter that they could not bear to part with her, keeping Martha under their roof in the secret room. In October 1918 Mr. Jones died in a hospital for wounded soldiers, from injuries sustained in France. His body was laid to rest at Wilford Hill Cemetery, whilst his widow plunged into a life of loneliness, burdened with a secret that she could never reveal. She could never remarry; never have more children to fill the void that tore at her for a lifetime. Imprisoned in her secret hell, unable to ask for help, unable to share her burden, she died, haunted, in the final weeks before her house was to be demolished.

The Council arranged a funeral for baby Martha Jones, and Mam insisted that it was held in St. Patrick's Church down the Meadows, where Mr. and Mrs. Jones had been married, in the glorious spring of 1914, where Martha had been baptised and where Mrs. Jones had attended Mass every Sunday morning. McCall and I received special leave from school to attend the funeral. I remember the people I saw weep at her wake weeping openly at the funeral of her child. Father Martin spoke of the immense sadness that had consumed Mrs. Jones and that now she was at peace. I remember thinking that God must have been happy that they were reunited as a family, as the morning sunshine tumbled through the magnificent stained glass windows. The sunlight illuminated the Christ who comforted the ivory-white children basking in his love, as rays of gold, crimson and blue light cascaded down, rippling in pools of molten colour on the floor. Mam wouldn't let go of me, especially when they were lowering Martha's small coffin into the equally small hole above her parents.

Next day Mam put in a request to be re-housed. Things moved pretty quickly. By Christmas we moved into a new house in Clifton and it was all change: a new school, new neighbours. Mam was pleased to be away from the McCall's, who lived up to expectations and became petty criminals of repute. Dad hated Clifton as there were only a handful of pubs, miles apart. I was reunited with my old school friends who remain my best pals to this day. Clifton was a short walk to Wilford Hill Cemetery so I would visit their grave and sit with them. I still do when I visit Mam, who's only a few yards away. I like to think of them looking after her. I was up there this morning tending to both graves. Mum's gravestone has very little on it, just her details, with lots of space for Dad me and our Theresa when our time comes. I like reading the Jones's gravestone and can't help but feel like our adventure, so long ago, brought them back together.

"William Jones. Born 27th February 1892, died October 1918. Charlotte Jones. Born 4th June 1895, died 12th September 1974. Martha Jones. Born 18th January 1916, died 5th March 1916. Reunited for eternity."

Squatters' Rites
Tom Johnstone

Flyboy takes three minutes to answer his bedroom door. As I stand there listening to the metallic clanging shaking the house, I wonder if he still has what I could think of as hands; wonder also if his head will still look the way it did the last time I saw it. I was still tripping then. I'm fairly certain I'm not now. I stare at the 'Section 666' he's pinned to his door. Double-protection from intrusion, along with the pentagram painted underneath. Will it protect us from the men outside hammering at the front door? Flyboy seems to think so, judging by his lackadaisical response to their knocking.

I knock again. I try to time it so it echoes the banging on the steel doors outside. Neither Flyboy's tongue-in-cheek Satanism, nor his collection of Famous Nutters of Filmland action figures -- Freddy, Jason, Leatherface, Michael Myers -- will repel the intruders, any more than the 'Section 6' legal notice in the front window. I've a feeling the heavies outside don't give a flying fuck about the legal niceties of the situation.

"We need a few extra bodies out front!" I call through the door. "We've got company…"

I hear him shuffling towards the door. I think of the cartoon murals with which he's decorated the house's peeling, magnolia wallpaper. They have a ribald garishness that reminds me of Robert Crumb, so vivid I could have sworn I saw them moving

141

last night. One has the caption "Oi! Bailiff! Make my day!" next to the head of a bailiff split open by an axe as if it were a log. The axe was visibly hacking away at it last night. Another shows a CCTV camera burnt at the stake, a veiny, organic-looking eyeball, sweating, bursting from its camera lens as the flames lick up its metal neck, flames that flickered last night, globules of hectic sweat that trickled down the cross-hatched optic nerve.

You wouldn't think so to look at his cartoons, but Flyboy's the gentlest person you could meet.

I remember the time some of the people in one of our previous squats had a Ketamine party. I've always thought that was a contradiction in terms. I walked through the front door and there was Flyboy, crawling aimlessly on his hands and knees along the dusty bare floor-boards of the corridor, his default grin plastered onto his face, a glazed expression in the pale blue eyes magnified by his thick lensed glasses. They looked like bug eyes even then. That's why we christened him Flyboy. That and the worn-out ex-RAF jacket he wears.

After what seems like an age, he opens the door. No wonder it took him so long. There must be thousands of door handles visible to him.

He's always seemed an innocent, bumbling figure. He still does, even now his head's taken up by two dinner plate sized eyes, each one with a convex, grid-like mesh dividing it up into countless minuscule eye-lets. And even now I've come down from the mushrooms, in the cold light of day, that's still a hairy, disc-like proboscis hanging from where his permanent grin used to sit.

The hammering from outside echoes through the carpetless, steel-shuttered house.

I lead him through the darkened corridors to the first-story, front-room bay window, where Natalie is trying to reason with the men banging on the steel door.

As far as I can gather from the exchange, the steel shutters and

142

doors are the reason for the onslaught from outside. The three big, mean-looking blokes trying to break the door down aren't bailiffs, police or the landlord's heavies. They're the fitters and probably the owners of all the hardware that should have kept the place squatter-proof. Our presence here is an affront to their craft, which isn't making them very friendly towards us.

"If you've damaged our kit…"

"But we haven't," insists Natalie.

One of the younger men lets out an ugly laugh.

"Then, why can't I unlock the fucking door?" the oldest of them demands, a man with shoulder-length grey hair, probably the younger one's father.

He waves a key as if it was a fist.

I don't like to tell him that I've jammed a piece of thick, wiry cable inside the lock. That was all I could do to secure the place. You can't exactly change the locks on one of these steel doors, at least not without some serious power tools, like welding equipment, maybe even oxy-acetylene torches. Things we don't have. When he tries the key again, ramming it in furiously, I worry that he will push the cable out. When the younger ones start banging and shoulder-barging the door again, I expect the force of the blows to knock it out. But the sinewy cable's jammed in pretty firmly. I can almost feel their frustration that the door's not giving way. There's a wealth of unspent fury in those men, which I'm sure they'll relish lavishing on our bodies if they ever do get through the door.

I look at Natalie. She's still got the whiskers sprouting from her white-furred cheeks. Her dark eyes are the same though, apart from the vertical slits of the pupils. The expression in them is human enough to make me wonder what my face looks like. And to worry about what she might think about it.

"Say something," she hisses. She breathes, hard. It whistles through her two sharp canine teeth. Or should that be feline teeth?

"Why doesn't she say something?" I wonder.

When did I become the Leader? I have enough trouble deciding things for myself, never mind doing it for anyone else.

The banging stops. Now there's a creaking of straining metal.

"Crowbar!" barks the patriarch of the firm, surgeon-style.

I look outside again. The men have given up trying to batter the steel door down. They are using a crowbar to try to prise it open.

After all, it worked for us.

I look down at them.

"Mate. Look. Seriously. What are you even going to do once you've got in here?"

The older man stops crow-barring for a moment. Looks up at me slowly.

"First I'm going to rip off that mask you're wearing," he says softly. "Then I'm going start on what's underneath…"

"Oh," I say. He carries on trying to lever the door open. "You know that's assault, don't you?" I add. "Have you read the legal notice in the window?"

My voice is drowned out by the younger men's mean, mirthless laughter. I don't think it would cut much ice anyway, even if they had read it. Thinking about the 'mask', my hand goes to my face. I feel the rough, regular pattern, the nose reduced to slit-like nostrils. My tongue takes over, exploring the scales. It shoots out. I can see its odd, crimson shape now, like a devil's toasting fork.

I don't have time to think about this now. The creaking strains caused by the crowbar are changing in timbre. It suggests that the men outside are about to make a breakthrough. Will my improvised lock-jam hold? I look down.

The lock-jam's academic. They're trying to prise the steel door-frame away from the building's own wooden one.

"There's about twenty of us in this place," I lie. "The rest'll be

144

here in a minute…"

The men outside laugh again. Weight of numbers is no deterrent to them, even if it weren't an empty threat.

There's certainly room for twenty people to live in this building, a former hostel for homeless addicts, empty for years apart from a brief period occupied by another crew of squatters, one of whom was Natalie. But it's been a few days since the three of us got in here, and the expected stampede of people rushing to take the empty rooms has not happened.

"Do something!" hisses Natalie, her pink nostrils twitching furiously.

The crowbar causes an agonised creak its holder's grunts echo.

"Bolt croppers!" he barks. He's going to snip the sinewy cable holding the steel doorframe in place, the same kind of cable I used to jam the lock.

Even though Natalie looks different, I still feel the same way about her, enough not to want to let her down. Maybe because she looks different. The feline look suits her.

Is it my wish to shine in her eyes that causes my tongue to shoot out of the window, returning with the jemmy gift-wrapped in the red ribbon of its forked end?

Flashbacks From Yesterday PM. #1.

In the darkness, I can't be sure which room is mine. Why is it pitch-black in late afternoon? I remember the doorway that gives out onto a small balcony and would provide light, but it's covered by one of those fucking steel security doors. Must get some air, some light. I feel sick, with the first nausea of the Liberty Caps taking hold. It isn't called 'psychotropic poisoning' for nothing. I looked them up in a book on fungal foraging. You have to really. A guy I knew on a road protest camp nearly saved the Department of Transport the cost of an eviction by serving some of the other residents Death Caps for breakfast. Hospital stomach pumps brought them back from the brink of death, while a skeleton-crew held the fort for a few desperate hours, just like we're keeping the bailiffs at bay here. I turn the steel handle and a metallic shriek echoes through the empty house. The light floods in, floods my senses, stained green, filtered through the membrane of the miniature jungle now growing from the black roofing-felt.

That wasn't there this morning.

"I see you planted up the balcony," I say to Natalie, after the men outside have fled. The tongue that swooped down and snatched their crowbar must have made them realise that our animal heads weren't cheap Halloween masks, just as I real-ised that they're not the remnants of yesterday's hallucinogens. Their bravado quickly turned to terror. We're just carrying on as normal, chatting about everyday things. Flyboy's not saying much of course, but he rarely does, apart from when he gets stoned and goes off on one about one of his conspiracy theories.

"What?" Natalie replies. She stares back at me blankly, her cat's face inscrutable. The crowbar lies on the dusty floor in front of us to remind us how things have suddenly changed.

She seems preoccupied. She often seems preoccupied. Hardly surprising really.

But it must have been her. She's the only gardener among us. Maybe she was tripping when she planted it up and can't remem-ber doing it.

"Where's Skunk then?" I ask her.

"Still in bed," she says.

I wonder what head Skunk's got now, which bed he's in. Hers, presumably.

"Shame," I say. "Could have done with an extra body out here."

Whatever head he has.

Got to get out.

146

The fish-flesh grey light creeps in. I step towards its source, the bay window, still open from our discussion with our would-be illegal evictors.

There's a strobing, blueish tinge to the light, I notice, faint crackling from the end of the street, tinny, sober, sobering voices.

Figures in fluorescent yellow jackets waving people away.

Police cars and barriers shutting off the end of the street.

Both ends of the street.

Flashbacks From Yesterday PM. #2.

Right, that's enough air: light fading now anyway, as though bleeding into the green foliage. I can feel the jungle growing up around me, sinuous vines or perhaps even snakes winding around my legs. Beneath me, in the garden of the next door house, I see a little girl, a tiny figure with luminous white-blonde curls and shining fairy wings, playing in the dirt outside. If she looks up and sees me, she might talk to me, and I might start acting Psilocybin-weird, so time to go back inside, into the welcoming, echoing blackness, where a thousand, smiling eyes might wait, the ones I've been looking for ever since the first time I saw them in the Liberty Caps' haze. As I turn to go, I see the little girl's mother snatch something from her tiny, porcelain hand. Then she glares up at me, shouts "Hey!" after me, waving the small, sharp, shiny object.

Too late. I pull the screaming tomb door shut behind me, drowning her protests that threaten to snare me like one of the snaking vines. I stumble around the landing, trying to remember which one is my door. There should be some light in there, electric or even natural, because no steel shutters cover my bedroom window. They only used them for the ground-floor doors and windows, and the upstairs door onto the balcony. If the light becomes unbearable, I could always stick a blanket up to restore the soothing darkness where I can hunt out comforting, twinkling eyes.

Is it this door?

Not sure.

Try it anyway.

"Sorry," I mumble, my voice crawling up through my throat's foggy tunnel, as I see Natalie straddling the bundled figure on her bed, though I dimly know that the act her mouth is performing on the figure's blotchy, red smear of a head isn't a sexual one.

She doesn't seem aware of me.

Natalie has already taken the trouble to hang curtains. Either that or she's opted for a room that already had them, left behind by previous occupants, tenants or squatters. She might even have put them up when she was here before. Whatever the reason, it's keeping the light out, so I can search for the little eyes that twinkle at me benevolently.

Even they aren't enough to take the edge off what's happening now.

It's hard to see them here in this ramshackle town house, where the peeling wallpaper turns to rotting flesh when I trip; they're stronger in the dark of country lanes and woods and foot-paths, where the voice of their consciousness sighs to me from hedgerows and gorse bushes.

The kiss Nat is giving to the blurry figure is purely practical in nature, a life-saver, I tell myself. This isn't just wishful thinking on my part: She breaks off from the mouth to mouth to interlock her fingers over his breast-bone. I remember she's a trained nurse. She pressed down frantically on his barrelled chest. To me, it almost looks as if she's pummelling him reproachfully. The motion begins to make her head as blurred as his, like she is changing.

"You can't bring Sam back that way," I say, the words flowing out of my mouth in a slow stream, one that's coming out with too much force for me to dam it, though I wish I could.

"This isn't Sam, you crazy bitch!" she screams, and something in me caves in, as Sam's head must have done when the grab's jaws closed around it. She stares at me for a moment, her breath slowing, until I look away. Then she carries on with the CPR and mouth-to-mouth, repeating the ritual until a dam bursts inside the figure's throat, releasing black ooze from within.

Yes, it looks nothing like Sam, the big, blobby body on the dusty floor. Sam was quite skinny. Also, unlike Sam, this body has a head, and is breathing now its airways are clear. And the head Sam did have was shaved, not covered in dirty blond dreadlocks like the ones now floating in the poisonous gunk Skunk's just coughed up. Nat shoves Skunk into the recovery position, leaves him breathing stertorously, comes over to me, arms outstretched. I don't want her pity though, so I stiffen in her hug, as she apologises for her harsh words.

I say "That's all right," a little grudgingly, and apologise back to her for mistaking this newcomer for her ex, the one she was with when she lived here before.

I suppose, even in the haze of my trip, it still filtered through that we owed her for helping us to get in here. We'd used her knowledge of the building from before, to enter and secure it, if you could call it secure.

The thing that bothered me was how she could bring herself to move back in here, with all the awful memories it held. I suppose that's why I said that thing about bringing Sam back, as crazy and tactless as it sounded. Was she really just trying to bring Skunk out of his smack overdose? Or was she doing something else? To my tripping eyes, it had looked like a rite; perhaps it really was one.

Not consciously maybe. She's the down-to-earth type, not one of your typical Brighton hippies. No bells or books or scented candles for her.

Speaking of which, where are all the Brighton hippies and punks and whatnot? Seems like they're steering clear of this place. Flyboy said he'd heard a lot of people would sooner sleep rough even in this freezing weather than spend a night in here. But then that's the kind of thing Flyboy would say.

Would have said rather, when he still had a mouth, rather than a proboscis Even then he probably wouldn't have said much anyway, just turned back to whatever William Burroughs he was reading at the time.

I'm beginning to think they were right to stay away.

When the shutter-men fled, I thought the siege had lifted, but the police cordons mean it's intensified. They must have babbled their story to the authorities. How will we eat? A fly buzzes around the window, bewildered by the invisible barrier of the pane, trapped like we are. My mouth waters, my tongue stirs, ready to shoot out and snatch the tiny insect. Then I see Flyboy, and stop myself.

I feel a hand gently laid on my shoulder, a whisker tickling my scaly cheek. I shiver, gasp.

"Were you tripping your tits off yesterday, Helen?" Nat asks, eyes narrowed.

"Might have been," I say.

"You were right though," says Nat. "I can't bring Sam back…"

I don't know if she's just making conversation. In any case, that's not what I said, but I don't like to point it out.

I'm surprised she's not talking about the changes that have come over me, or at least, my face. Mind you, I haven't commented on hers either. A bit like how I didn't say anything about the way Skunk's pin-prick pupils seemed to be disappearing beneath his drooping eyelids when she introduced us yesterday, though I felt like saying, "You really know how to pick them, Nat." It's as if we've made an unspoken agreement not to mention our new faces, how and why they've changed in this way.

150

"…But maybe I can do something to get the bastards back," she says, her voice a low, menacing purr.

I wonder which bastards she means: the company that skimped on health and safety measures, the employment agency that sent Sam there, the dole office that threatened to stop his money if he didn't register with the agency. He'd only been there a few hours when it happened. There'd been no banksman employed in the dock warehouse, no one to watch the machine and direct its operator, no one to warn him that Sam's head was in the way when its huge, steel jaws closed. I heard about the accident when I came to return a bag of tools I'd borrowed from Nat. It was a good excuse to see her, even though I knew she and Sam were an item. The time before, when I'd come to get the tools, she'd been out and he'd been there. I'd ended up going to bed with him. That wasn't what I'd meant to do. Maybe I'd thought I'd smell her on him or something. Yes, maybe that was the real reason. Maybe I'd fucked him as some sort of rite, to join me to her indirectly if not actually.

When I brought the tools back a few days later, she was there and he wasn't. The police were with her. Squatters mostly talk to coppers through the letterbox if they talk to them at all, they don't tend to invite them in. Yet here they were. Nat was sobbing, and Sam wasn't there. He wasn't coming back.

Flashbacks From Yesterday PM. #3.

Darkness is falling by the time I find my bed and tumble into it, staring at the ceiling to try to summon up the eyes of the dark, to hear whatever strange intelligence guides them, whisper soothing words to me. I see the oddly scrawled drawing up there by the fading light from the curtain-less, unshuttered window. I noticed it before, yet I haven't looked at it properly until now. My eyes begin to follow the crudely scribbled black curves to see what they form. I see arms, legs, a body lolling there on the grey plaster, a bulbous, red mess where the head might be. A cartoon-ish, popping eye on a protruding stalk.

I lower my eyes. Pieces of plaster lie scattered on the floor. I look up at the source of this mess, a hole in the wall where the branch of a tree outside has grown through from the neglected garden, unchecked by pruning secateurs.

It felt weird, seeing her like that, tearfully accepting the police officer's condolences, wanting to help console her myself, yet not feeling up to the task. I'd loved him too, though briefly and hurriedly. I was grieving too. She had a longer time with him to mourn, more memories of him than the fishy, rubbery smell of a tied-up condom with a white blob inside.

Yet I would have been happy to become the shoulder for her to cry on, if only she'd have let me. Too soon, I suppose. And I didn't feel I knew her well enough. She seemed to have closer friends rallying round. I left her there in that room, the one that's somehow ended up being mine.

Who drew that horrible picture on the ceiling, like some dis-turbed child's blown-up sketch of a nightmare?

It's certainly not up to Flyboy's standards. And anyway, he wasn't here when the first lot of squatters were in residence, like she was.

"What did you have in mind?" I ask. "Another protest? A lot of good the last one did."

In the days following Sam's death, there were occupations of the local Job Centre and the employment agency in question. In the dockyard where the tragedy took place, cranes were forced to cease work for the day by demonstrators scaling them and hanging garishly coloured banners. After a while, people started to drift away from the protests as they became more repetitious, those remaining just going through the motions, chanting slogans like church-goers mouthing hymns.

"I know," she says, her whiskers twitching with what looked like irritation: thin, vertical pupils regarding me coolly. "I was there, remember?"

"So was I." (I went along to support Nat. So did quite a few others.) "I remember that banner you made on that sheet, the one with 'MURDERERS' on it?"

"Yeah, I just slapped it on with thick, black paint."

"Not very subtle."

"But effective. Got in all the papers, hanging from some cooling tower, or whatever it was. What happened to it, d'you know?"

"Kept turning up at various protests like a bad penny. You could use it for almost anything."

"Anything where someone had died and someone was to blame," she amended. "Funny how after the first week, people got bored and moved onto something else…"

"Or maybe they just had to get on with their lives."

"Unlike me, you mean?"

I sigh.

"No, I didn't mean… Sorry, that wasn't meant to come out like that."

I keep thinking she's going to say, "Did you fuck him?" But she doesn't know. I think so anyway. Yes, I think she really doesn't know.

I see her looking at the catch my lizard's tongue has landed. The crow-bar.

Is she thinking of a more forceful payback? Something that might shut the firm responsible down for more than a day? How does she think we're going to get past the police cordons at either ends of the street? Maybe she hasn't thought of that.

Skunk stumbles in, asking what's going on in his low, gruff

mumble. She really does pick them. I could sort of see the attraction of Sam, hence my quick tumble with him: I just wanted to find out what all the fuss was about. That hasty grapple on the mattress was enough to remind me why I tend to go for my own sex. Not that he wasn't gentle in his way, certainly compared to some. As for this one, Skunk... Well, let's put it this way, I don't need to try it to know I don't want to buy it.

With a sinking feeling, I see Skunk has the head of a lion with the same dirty-orange, dread-locked mane, though his pupils are needle-points. I think of the hypodermic he must have tossed carelessly into the next-door garden for the neighbours' kid to play with.

"Heavies trying to break in," I say. "All over now though..."

He whistles through his heavy jaw as he sees the crow-bar. He crouches down to examine it. Is he thinking how much he could get for it? Enough for a fix, for another of his rituals of self-negation?

My tongue shoots out to snatch it away.

"Jesus, Helen!" he rasps.

"Hands off," I hiss. "Finders, keepers. Anyway, look outside. The heavies have gone, but we've still got company. Police. Or maybe not."

I lead him to the bay windows. But the police have gone, the regular police anyway. There are others there now. The vans parked at each end of the road are white, unmarked, not even registration plates on them. Beside them stand faceless figures, fully covered in white suits, with masks, carrying what look like guns.

I look at Flyboy. I remember him talking about the special ops group he reckoned existed to deal with paranormal events. I thought it was just the usual stoned bollocks he came out with, all the Illuminati conspiracy bullshit.

A siren is going off, making a shrill noise I've never heard before, like a car alarm on crack. I look at the figures at the end of the street. In their white hazmat suits, they don't look like people at all, more like ghosts, or KKK members. And those things they're carrying that look like guns: flame-throwers?

Outside the sky no longer looks like fish-flesh. More like fish-skin, or the scales on my new face. The sun appears from time to time behind these flecks of mackerel cloud. Soon it will disappear behind the buildings across the street, such as the Chinese takea-way where we went for chips last night. We won't be going there tonight, never mind to the dockyard. I remember something Flyboy said, his bug eyes staring into mine through his thick lenses, before his eyes were literally those of a bug, the thing he told me about the hazmat men. He said they do their main work at night. But what work? What hazardous materials are they here to remove? Is it us? Or whatever substances have brought about the changes in us?

Maybe they don't make much of a distinction when it comes down to it.

Maybe they're not choosy about where to aim those guns or flame-throwers or whatever they are.

"Come on," I say. I think of the branch piercing the wall of my room. What we must do suddenly hits me, like a blow from that crow bar. I grab Natalie's hand. "Let's get out of here," I say.

"Where?" she asks, demands. "Where can we go? The whole street's cordoned off, Helen."

"I know," I say.

I lead her out of the room overlooking the street. I don't see if the others follow. It doesn't matter, so long as she's with me, though I don't want to leave Flyboy behind. On the darkened landing, where wallpaper hangs like corpse skin or rotting veg-etation, the tiny little eyes are there, drifts of them steering me towards the steel door onto the balcony. I guide Natalie and the others towards the jungle outside that I know will now be vast, an emerald world for us, where things will be different.

"Look," I say. "See where it's breaking through into our world already!"

Natalie doesn't react to the huge, gnarled tree trunk bursting through the damp wallpaper. Can't she see the forest she planted? It's hard to tell what Flyboy can see with his compound eyes.

I feel her hesitation.

"Come on, Nat," I coax her. "He'll be there, I know it…"

"Who?" she asks. "Helen, what are you talking about?"

"Sam," I say.

I think of him in that strange green light, filtered by lush chlorophyll, resurrected for her. I hope he'll be whole again, his unruptured head back on his shoulders, not like in that horror story about the monkey's paw. I would do this for her, even though he might come between us. My love is unconditional. Better that than see her reduced to playing handmaiden to a junky.

She breaks free from my grasp and takes a step back from me, as I turn the screeching handle. I throw open the door to reveal the vast forest that stretches out beyond.

The Writers

In 1988 GRAHAM JOYCE gave up his job in international youth work and set off in a red and white 2CV to travel across Europe to live on the Greek Island of Lesbos. It was there in a scorpion infested beach shack that he wrote and sold his first novel *Dreamside*. He went on to write a further nineteen novels and numerous short stories. During his writing career he won many literary prizes including the British Fantasy Award, the World Fantasy Award for best novel and the prestigious O. Henry Prize for best short story. *Tiger Moth* was inspired by a childhood encounter with two boys when he was on holiday in Norfolk. Graham died in 2014 aged 59.

EMMA J. LANNIE was born in Manchester and now lives in Derby. Her first short story collection *Behind A Wardrobe In Atlantis* was published in 2014 by Mantle Lane Press. A founder member of literature collective Hello Hubmarine, she helps run Derby Writers' Hub, organises spoken word and live literature events, leads workshops, and drinks a shedload of tea. Emma is currently working on her novel *The Path From You Back To Me*. She has had writing published in After The Fall, Overheard, 100RPM, Jawbreakers, Scattered Reds, Bugged, Even More Tonto Short Stories, Dzanc Best Of The Web 2010, 6SV1, Tripod, and in various places online including 3:AM, Kill Author and Straight From The Fridge.

ANNABEL BANKS has an MA in prose and is nearing completion of her practice-based poetry PhD. Her work can be found in numerous journals and anthologies, and has won or been nominated for a number of awards. She is currently working on a novel about social manipulation called *I Can Help You Live*.

WILLIAM GALLAGHER is a Birmingham-born writer of Doctor Who radio scripts, Radio Times reviews and BBC News Online columns. He also got fired off Crossroads but doesn't like talking about that. He'd rather you knew about *The Beiderbecke Affair*, a book he wrote for the British Film Institute and *The Blank Screen*, a guide for writers who need to be more productive. His work has also appeared regularly in Radio Times magazine and BBC News Online plus The Independent, the Los Angeles Times and on BBC local and national radio. He once had afternoon tea on a Russian nuclear submarine and regrets calling the place a dive.

BRIAN ENNIS is a writer, teacher, gamer and geek from Peterborough, England. He writes dark, miserable fiction and fun, humorous articles, because he's always of two minds about everything. His fiction has been published by Sanitarium Magazine, The Colored Lens, Niteblade, and Theme of Absence. He writes articles for Dirge Magazine and reviews for the British Fantasy Society, and is a founder member of the Critical Twits gaming podcast. He still doesn't know what he wants to be when he grows up.

RICHARD FARREN BARBER was born in Nottingham in July 1970. After studying in London he returned to the East Midlands. He lives with his wife and son and works as a Registry Manager for a local university. He has written over 200 short stories and has had short stories published in Alt-Dead, Alt-Zombie, ePocalypse – Tales from the End, Horror D'Oeuvres, Murky Depths, Midnight Echo, Midnight Street, Morpheus Tales, Night Terrors II, Siblings, The House of Horror, Trembles, When Red Snow Melts, and broadcast on The Wicked Library, Tales to Terrify and Pseudopod. Richard's novella, *The Power of Nothing* was published by Damnation Books in 2013 and his next novella, *The Sleeping Dead* was published in 2014 by DarkFuse.

LIZ KERSHAW lives in Herefordshire and divides her time between writing, working on the family smallholding , working with vulnerable young people and training to be a counsellor. She writes short stories and historical crime fiction: her current novel-in-progress *The Burial of the Dead* is set in 1934. Liz won the M R Hall/PanMacmillan 'Best Opening of a Crime Story' competition (2012), the Bedford International Writing Competition (2015) and the No Exit Press, Crime Fiction Short Story competition (2015). She has had stories accepted for www.triptychtales.net and Fifty Flashes of Fiction. In 2014 she was accepted onto Writing West Midlands prestigious Room 204 programme for the best emerging writers in the Midlands area.

PASCALE PRESUMEY'S blood is French but her heart has taken root in the UK where she has been residing for years. She is a member of Room 204, Writing West Midlands' Writers Development Scheme and has had short stories published in various magazines both in the UK and North America. She is at present working on her second novel, *Battles Without Names*, about Hugo, a Compagnon du Devoir, an ancient craftsmen organisation known for their strict moral rules and bizarre initiation rituals. To complete his apprenticeship, Hugo must complete one more 'tour' and go work for a renowned master craftsman in a small village in Yorkshire. It is March 1984 and the Miners Strike is about to begin.

FIONA JOSEPH has authored two books inspired by the Cadbury chocolate entrepreneurs from her home town of Birmingham, UK. Her biography *Beatrice: The Cadbury Heiress Who Gave Away Her Fortune* was long-listed in the Rubery Book Award, and chosen by the Alliance of Independent Authors and the Quaker Book Centre as their Book of the Month. Her latest story is *Comforts for the Troops*, a novel woven from the tales of Cadbury women workers during World War One. Fiona's short fiction has appeared in various anthologies. She won a prize in the Happenstance International Short Story Competition and was awarded the Prize for Fiction from Birmingham City University/National Academy of Writing whilst completing her Postgraduate Diploma in Writing.

RAY ROBINSON first won attention in 2006 with his debut novel, *Electricity*. It was shortlisted for both the James Tait Black Memorial Prize and the Authors' Club First Novel Award. Robinson's other novels are *The Man Without* (2008), *Forgetting Zoe* (2010), and *Jawbone Lake* (2014). Robinson is a post-graduate of Lancaster University, where he was awarded a Ph.D. in Creative Writing in 2006, and is a Mentor for The Literary Consultancy. He has appeared at literary festivals around the world, including La Feria Internacional del Libro de Guadalajara, Mexico, and the Edinburgh International Book Festival.

REEN JONES lives in Northamptonshire with three cats and an over-draft. She completed a course in Creative Writing a couple of years ago, and at present concentrates on short stories in the horror/speculative fiction genre, while working part time. She dreams of one day producing that fantastically successful novel, which will enable her to use the proceeds to retire to the dark side of the moon and open a bar.

JAY SEATE claims that after reading a few of his stories, his parents booted him out of the house. He became a guitarist in a band, sold artwork and freelanced for various photo publications until finishing college and then surviving the Southeast Asian conflict. After raising a family and sneaking through a career as an investigator, Jay was again bitten by the writing bug which is his current passion. Winner of Horror Novel Review's 2013 Best Short Fiction Award, Jay writes everything from humor to the erotic to the macabre, and is especially keen on transcending genre pigeonholing. Over two hundred stories have appeared in magazines, anthologies and webzines. Jay lives in Golden, Colorado with the dream of enjoying the rest of his life travelling and writing.

FRAN HILL is a 50-something year old writer and English teacher from Warwickshire, England. She writes fiction, articles and poetry, and her first book *Being Miss*, a comedy, charts a rollercoaster day in a teacher's life. Her writing on education and English studies appears in TES, the weekly magazine for teachers, and in emag, a magazine for A level students. She writes funny bespoke poetry for special occasions and sometimes performs her work on stage with the help of a small brandy.

SCOTTY CLARK produced the award winning documentary *Evidently ... John Cooper Clarke* which was broadcast on BBC4. With a full time job, a young family and a love of Notts County FC, Scotty experiences literature poverty, in that he has to either read or write, as he doesn't have enough time to do both to the extent he'd like. Scotty is now coming towards the end of a reading period and he is excited about his next writing phase. *Mrs. Jones' House* is his first short story and he plans to deliver more before starting his first novel. Should he ever win the lotto, he would revel in giving his day job up so he could both read and write with equal application.

TOM JOHNSTONE'S fiction has appeared in various publications, including the ninth, tenth and eleventh Black Books of Horror, (Mortbury Press), *Brighton – The Graphic Novel* (Queenspark Books),

Supernatural Tales 27 & 31, *Wicked Women* (Fox Spirit Books), *Shroud Magazine15* and *Strange Tales V* (Tartarus Press). As well as these writing credits, he co-edited the British Fantasy Award-nominated austerity-themed anthology *Horror Uncut: Tales of Social Insecurity and Economic Unease* with the late Joel Lane, published September 2014, by Gray Friar Press. He lives in Brighton with his partner and two children. He works as a gardener for the local authority.

Links

Annabel Banks	www. annabelbanks.com
Richard Farren Barber	www.richardfarrenbarber.co.uk
William Gallagher	www.williamgallagher.com
Fran Hill	www.franhill.co.uk
	www.ilurveenglish.blogspot.com
Tom Johnstone	www. tomjohnstone.wordpress.com
Fiona Joseph	www.fionajoseph.com
Graham Joyce	www.grahamjoyce.co.uk
Liz Kershaw	www.lizkershaw.co.uk
Emma J. Lannie	www.garglingwithvimto.blogspot.co.uk
Ray Robinson	www.rayrobinsonwriter.weebly.com
J. T. Seate	www.troyseateauthor.webs.com
The Dunce	www.thedunce.co.uk
Mantle Lane Press	www.mantlelanepress.co.uk
	www.red-lighthouse.org.uk

Acknowledgements

This publication was supported using public funding by the National Lottery through Arts Council England

Mantle Lane Press would like to acknowledge support from Writing East Midlands and Writing West Midlands.

Thanks to Sue Joyce for permission to include *Tiger Moth*.

Mantle Lane Press is a subsidiary of Mantle Arts Limited, which receives financial support from North West Leicestershire District Council.

Supported using public funding by
ARTS COUNCIL ENGLAND
LOTTERY FUNDED